Scurry
County
Style

Scurry County Style

Stories from below the Cap Rock and beyond

By Viola M. Payne

Introduction by Thomas B. Whitbread

UNIVERSITY OF TEXAS PRESS AUSTIN & LONDON

Library of Congress Catalog Card No. 67–27371
Copyright © 1967 by Viola M. Payne
All Rights Reserved

Printed in the United States of America
by the Printing Division of The University of Texas, Austin
Bound by Universal Bookbindery, Inc., San Antonio

To Travis

Acknowledgments

In this space it is not possible to list all the persons who have encouraged and helped me with my writing during my lifetime. First of all my parents, Susan and Barney L. Autry, were sources of interest and inspiration. My dad was a wonderful storyteller who knew many details of nature and Southwestern life, and he took time from a life of hard work to share them with me. My mother loved poetry, music, and fine literature, and from her I developed a yearning to accomplish something in the arts. Although they were poor in the material things of this world, this couple left a memory of courage and devotion that amazes me more with each passing year. Relatives on both sides of our closely-knit families contributed much, including Grandfather Jacob Brown Autry and Uncle Corley Bozeman. My sisters—Rowena (Moitoret), Katherine (Talbot), and Frances (Jones) —my brother, Jacob Autry, and his wife, Wanda, cousins Alice Todaro, and others were always ready with assistance. Valuable counsel was found in Snyder, Texas, from English teacher Margaret Dell Pilcher, and friends Louise Blanchard, Frances Brooks, Sally O'Rear, Elizabeth Beavers. And nothing could have been accomplished without the understanding of my husband, Travis, as well as that of my children. In El Paso, Helen Sellers, Alyce Bennett, and the entire El Paso Writer's League have contributed much time to my efforts.

A number of friends contributed directly to the making of this book, including members of the National Amateur Press Association. Particular credit is due Dr. Thomas Whitbread, professor of English at The University of Texas, who first suggested the compiling of these stories, and spent much time weeding material and arranging it into a meaningful presentation. Among the stories chosen were a number which were first set in type by members of the National Amateur Press Association, an organization devoted to artistic writing and printing, in the following publications: *The Victorian*, Victor A. Moitoret, editor; *Far Afield*, F. F. Thomas, Jr., editor; *The Fossil*, Edward H. Cole, editor; *Literary Newsette*, Willametta Keffer, editor; *The Martini*, Martin Keffer, editor; *Rays*, Ray Allen Albert, editor; *Spectator*, Milton R. Grady, editor; *Scarlet Cockerel*, Ralph Babcock, editor; *Reverie*, Robert Telschow, editor; *Amateur of Shenandoah*, J. Rolfe Castelman, editor.

"The Red Geranium" was published in the magazine the *Youth's Instructor* (June 1, 1965), by the Review and Herald Publishing Company, with Walter Crandall as editor. This story won a first prize in the Pen League Division of this magazine.

Viola M. Payne
El Paso, Texas

Introduction

For nearly twenty years stories and narratives by Viola M. Payne have delighted perceptive readers in the National Amateur Press Association, as well as in her native Texas. It is thoroughly right that this volume of her work now appear.

Viola Payne, in her own words, "actually went to school from the common people of Scurry County—and the out-of-doors." Her stories "belong to the rural people of the Colorado River country." She was born Viola Margaret Autry in Cuthbert, Mitchell County, Texas. "Grandparents on both sides were pioneers in the area—one grandfather surveyed the area and taught some of the first schools established there." For a short time she lived on a homestead in Rio Arriba County, New Mexico, and then returned to the family farm twenty miles southwest of Snyder, Texas. Her first schooling—the Bible, the dictionary, any other of the few books that could be borrowed—was "in a community schoolhouse known as 'County Line,' right where Scurry and Mitchell Counties meet." Married to Travis Payne in 1938, mother of a daughter and two sons, she now lives in El Paso.

A perennial critics' debate, how to cubbyhole invention and description as separate elements, cannot be resolved here, any more than it can with regard to almost any fiction. A few of Mrs. Payne's pieces seem clearly autobiographical at root. Some seem covertly so. Most of them seem to be crafted fictions based on experienced knowledge. All the pieces in this volume, whatever name you may wish to give them, display an observant eye, an ear as well tuned as Frost's or Twain's for local palavers, concomitant sharp detail and analogy, frequent humor, and humane compassion. Viola Payne loves her land and most of her fellow men—and delights, here, in telling of them.

Her land is mainly Scurry County (beneath the Cap Rock), but extends atop the Llano Estacado and beneath the Davis Mountains, and touches Fort Worth and Korea. Her people include adolescents of both sexes, country fiddlers, self-styled preachers, ranchers and farmers of many sorts, and a variety of father-mother husbands and wives. And she commands a distinctive, personal style. As a capsule instance of the quality of Mrs. Payne's perceptions and of her prose here is a vignette, "Threshold":

I finish an errand in town, and turn the red pickup homeward. As I climb low ridges toward the northwest, the morning is at an apex of dewy freshness.

Gone are the stricken days; no longer is a hostile sun fastened against a burning sky. Now it shines with a soft, diffused glow across each tender blade of grass. No more will cotton clasp two starving leaves in a prayer for rain. Rain has come with the south wind.

The south wind has slipped from the Gulf of Mexico and danced across the far-flung arms of the Brazos. She has routed red sandstorms and rolled thunderheads into the Concho country. She has cooled her feet in the waters of the Llano; she has stolen along in the light of the moon. She has run, laughing, through the new grass; she has trailed her bright hair across the plain. She has stirred the bony ridges of the Colorado, and tossed warm glances toward the cap-rocks. Mesquite has spun leaves across her pathway; cactus has flamed at her touch. Gulf clouds have rigged sails against her, and are bouncing forward into the sky of the north.

Suddenly, just around a curve, I come upon a herd of cattle being driven to new pastures. Older Herefords bawl, and baby calves side-step in swift terror. Sleek bodies graze the pickup, and dart back aganist the fence-row. Horsemen wave gaily and weave their mounts in and out; their soft voices soothe the noise of the cattle. Saddles creak and jingle; light flows across the rippling motions of the horses.

The road ahead becomes more complicated. Two long oil-trucks appear. They turn impatiently to one side and start lumbering through the russet sea of cattle. "Move over, Yesterday," they seem to say. "Make way for Tomorrow!"

The feel of this complex country, its landscape and its people —old Comanches remembered from before 1876, emigrant Mexicanos, high-plains Negro cotton pickers imported from East Texas, town-dwelling ranch-buying oil exploiters, and, most of all, the various individual slightly more native people of the West Texas country beneath the Cap Rock, at the button-willow-bottomed, farm-, ranch-, and mesquite-surrounded headwaters of the Concho, the Llano, the Colorado—these are what Viola Payne gives us in the fine stories of this book.

Thomas B. Whitbread
Austin, Texas

Contents

Claybourne Pastures

It was a warm morning, even for June, in the river country below the Cap Rock of western Texas. Young Davy Turnbow and his father, Preston, sauntered through the dappled shade of pecan trees along the valley joining the stream. Davy was a small carbon copy of his tall spare father, and he moved with the same light and easy stride. Across a shoulder of each was thrown a crooked willow pole.

Preston swatted at gnats swarming around his face, pushed back his brown felt hat, and mopped his sweat-streaked brow. His expression ranged between relief and eagerness. "I'll say, Davy." He spoke in a soft, even cadence. "Nobody will ever know how glad I am to get out of that blamed oil-field town. I would have rather died than raise you in that town, boy. Shows, shows, shows—moving-picture shows and fights—that's all boys know in that trashy part of town where we lived. I knew you'd never be any account if we kept you there."

Davy looked about him with the exultation of a young animal loosed from a cage. "Can I really go all over this river, Dad, with no one to stop me?"

"You bet your life!" Preston smiled. "I didn't save up money to buy the old home place for nothing! I grew up here, boy. I know every inch of this old river. I used to swing across on willow limbs right here."

He stepped toward the edge of the river bank, and a locust sounded under his feet. Davy sprang back quickly, dropped his pole, and began to run.

Preston raised his hand. "Come back here, son. Listen here," he added quietly, "you're a country boy now. You got to learn not to run ever time a little old locust-bug sounds."

"I thought it was a snake." The boy trembled slightly while he ventured back.

"A rattlesnake? No, boy—that sound was too shrill and loud. You take a old rattlesnake, he makes a soft, *whirr-rring* sound. You wouldn't likely find a rattlesnake this near the river noway. They like to stay back up in the rocks—in the roughs. You come on down this trail with me. You'll learn real quick."

Preston advanced down a cow trail to where a rusty fence sagged through the brush. "This fence is about to fall down." He frowned. "I got to fix it." He pushed down one strand of the wire. "Bend low, Davy. Don't tear your shirt."

The boy inched through. "Is this our land too, Daddy?"

"Oh no, boy. Not that it makes any difference. This is Claybourne land. Sixteen sections of it, across the river here. Claybournes bought it before I was born. It's the finest land in the country. I always said I'd rather own it than any."

"Then the Claybournes will be our neighbors? Do they have a boy our size?"

"Well, no—their boy is grown. And what's the pity of it, they don't live on the land. Never did. As long as I can remember, Claybournes have lived in town. They've kept cows, though, and always drove out here to see about them. Said this ranch was just an investment.

"People around here have sometimes been mad at the Claybournes. People said they were stuck-up, and shouldn't own land they didn't live on." Preston shook his head. "I don't know; Sam Claybourne was always real nice to me and my folks when I was growing up. He told me to go ahead and fish—never to ask. He told us to gather all the wild plums we wanted, and take dead mesquite whenever we wanted it." Preston looked about. "But look how this grass is beat down. See how those little red gullies are beginning to wash around the mesquite trees over there? There's been too many cows on this pasture. Claybournes must be getting careless. It's bad for land to have too many cows on it."

"How much farther do we go?"

"Right here." Their trail circled a limpid hole of blue-green water. "Watch for grasshoppers to bait your hook."

When the hooks were baited the man and boy sat under a pecan tree to watch them. They stayed motionless for some time, hearing only the call of a mourning dove from a faraway thicket.

"I don't believe this hole of water is as deep as it used to be," Preston whispered. He poked around the bank. "Look, I hit silt bottom. Wonder what made it fill up so?"

There was a stir through the willow trees around the bend. First the frothy head of a horse emerged, and then the set young face of a heavy man. He was a showily dressed stranger, with shiny black boots barely touched with dust. He rode to the bank above Preston, reined his horse, but made no move to dismount.

"Who gave you permission to fish here?" he asked.

Preston slowly rose, dusting the knees of his levis as he came up. "I don't believe I know you," he answered softly. "My name is Turnbow, and by home place joins this one on the north. I've known Sam Claybourne for as long as I live."

"Claybourne?" The man stared with pale eyes. "And what makes you think Claybourne has anything to do with this outfit here? My name's Bud Ennis, and I own this ranch. I bought it last year."

Preston stood motionless. "I didn't know," he said. "I didn't dream Claybourne would ever sell. I just moved back to this country yesterday; I hadn't heard."

"Claybourne didn't want to sell." A laugh rippled across the muscles of Ennis' face without reaching his eyes. "He went broke in town. This ranch was all that ever kept him up, anyhow."

"But his son—his boy?" Preston faltered.

"Oh, him? He never stayed out here anyway. They sent him off to some school. He's off somewhere teaching agriculture now."

Preston pulled his line from the water and started rolling it on his pole. "Careful with your hook, Davy."

"You can tell your friends over there on those sandy-land farms," Ennis continued, "to stay off this place. I don't want my cattle bothered by hunting dogs, or people gathering pecans, plums, algeritas, or deadwood. I've made some money in the oil business and now I'm going to make some out of cattle."

Preston kept his voice even. "Maybe you'll build a home out here," he offered. "We would like to have some neighbors to the south."

Ennis laughed. "Build away out here? We're going to live in town where there's some place to go to. I told you I bought this thing to make money on."

"Davy, we'd best be going." Preston led the boy back down the trail.

Davy's feet dragged along, and he kept looking back. At last the fence boundary was reached. "We could hide here in the plum brush," he said. "We could hide here until he leaves, and then go back."

"No, Davy." His father lifted the wire again. "We don't go where we're not wanted."

"But I want to go back and fish! It was a pretty place. It was the prettiest place I ever saw. I want to go back!"

"Not today, Davy," Preston answered gently. "We'll have to wait awhile."

Prelude

The Texas moon had crested the ridge above Pecan Creek when Bert Westfall edged his car into the sharp crossing. Water gurgled against the worn tires on each wheel.

In the button willows fringing the still water night insects were beginning a sweet, sibilant song. Grass stretched away from the creek bank in a parklike expanse, and ended where a grove of pecan trees rustled sleepily.

Bert was in no hurry. He steered his car to one side, turned off the key, and stared straight ahead. Never mind if he was late to the musicale at Howard Payton's—he had been late to everything for weeks. How could a fellow get ready for anything on time with an unfinished fiddle tune and a brown-eyed girl all hopelessly mixed up in his mind?

A ray of moonlight crept on the weathered steering wheel and inched across Bert's face. It disclosed a round, generous countenance built to remain in a gentle mold. But now bewilderment clouded the mild brown eyes, and wrinkled his forehead. It caused Bert to run his fingers slowly through the dark fringe above his ears. Those fingers were the tapering, artistic kind, which always caused people to exclaim, "Are you *the* Bert Westfall from Pecan Creek who plays the violin?"

There was no use trying to think of a finish to the tune now. All he could think about was how he hoped Joyce would be at the musicale, even if Crockett Trevey brought her. She couldn't be too interested in Crockett. That dab of oil on his dad's land had ruined him for sure. She probably had figured that out in a minute.

Bert puzzled over what life had been like before Joyce Hazelwood had suddenly appeared from the Willow Grove community to visit a Pecan Creek party. He didn't even want to think about it! If only her dark hair and eyes wouldn't catch all those golden lights! Once, upon a dim porch, he had dared to look closely at her—and there had been a shine about her which stabbed the warm swirl of a reel into his chest. Why in the world did she have to be so slim and rounded and quick and graceful? Why didn't she have a shrill voice, instead of one with the tone of *D* note? The sound of it made him want to pick up his bow and start into a waltz.

A fellow more than thirty years old ought to have better sense. Here was he, Bert Westfall, who had never so much as noticed a girl in his life, acting in this miserable way! Always when other fellows got into romantic scrapes and went around suffering for months he was the one who teased a little and sat back at parties ironing out their dented hearts with his fiddle bow. As for fiddle playing—that time he had played for the amateur hour in Three Springs the whole town and stood up and screamed and yelled for more. That was the time he had taken the Mockingbird song and added thrush calls, mourning doves, chaparral, bobwhites and whippoorwills.

He spent most of his time on other things—farming cotton over where Pecan Creek made the bend just before it joined the river. He hadn't spent any time worrying about girls—until this funny, crazy thing had happened to him. He could have saved a lot of trouble by deciding on that square old maid who baked the good pecan pies for rabbit drives. But no—one glance from the corner of Joyce's dreamy eyes was worth more than all other women could offer.

But here—what was he doing wasting time dreaming above Pecan Creek? The Paytons couldn't start a musicale without him.

He reluctantly urged the car up the wash-boarded incline. It was odd about some families, such as the Treveys. They could have oil wells and build a fine house on the highway and still not have a bit of company. The Paytons lived in an old tumbledown house you had to cross two creeks to even find—yet people beat a well-worn trail to their front door. There was the house up ahead, leaning back against mesquite and desert-willow trees. Cars were parked all over the hill, and the house was so full of people they had spilled out across the porch and yard. Small boys had already jerked half the pickets out of the fence, and were chasing each other around every corner.

"Bert, get your slow self in here," Payton yelled from the steps. "We've been waiting on you an hour!"

Bert grinned. He dusted his drab jeans and red-striped shirt. He rummaged for his violin case. "Why don't you start something?"

"Start something without you?" This voice stopped him in his tracks. Bert swallowed. Joyce Hazelwood pressed out from the crowd. She moved in front of the withered morning-glory vines as artfully as if in a quadrille. Tonight she had on a skirt which was pleated all around, and yellow as the wings of a butterfly. Had Crockett Trevey brought her? There he stood—as straight and tall as a pecan sapling. His young features were even enough to have been carved from river rock. He casually reached over, took Joyce by the arm, and whispered something in her ear.

Bert addressed the congregation on the porch. "How many guitars you got tonight?"

"Three."

"Get 'em tuned up." Bert scraped his boots across a loose board on the porch and shook the candlebugs from the screen. He tossed his crumpled brown hat in a corner and nodded to everyone. He moved down the cane-reinforced line along one side of the room, and settled in a chair near the light.

"You in a playing notion tonight?" someone asked.

"I'm always in that notion." Bert hit *A* note for the assembling guitar players, and the room began to quiet.

There were other vacant chairs in the room, yet Joyce slipped up to the one right beside him, with Crockett tagging along behind her. She cupped her chin in her hands, and turned a disturbing gaze upon Bert. He felt that look move across and into his fingers.

"How did you learn to play?" she asked him.

He looked up from his strings. Learn to play? How did a boy happen to be born with a queer ache in his fingers which led him to rub two cottonstalks together until he could scrape together the money for a Sears Roebuck fiddle? And then the day when the package had come—and the bitter disappointment when the strings were tightened. A fiddle—but no teacher. Only jolting scratchings, scrapings, and squeaks. He had gone behind the corral to hide his hot tears. But soon he had washed his face and begun to try again. And then, a few days later, a norther had whistled around the house in the night. In the sounds there was a flurry of tones. He had strange impulses to capture them on the strings.

"Oh, I just sort of learned it all by myself," he answered. A tinge of red crept toward his ears.

"Wonderful!" Her voice slipped all the way down from the *D* string into harmonics. "You play beautifully—and I do mean beautifully. You ought to be famous."

"Oh, ma'am, I don't want to be famous." Bert shyly shook his head. "There are other things better."

Crockett yawned.

'How's your crops?" The question reached Bert from a foggy distance.

"It was pretty fair till about three weeks ago." Bert jarred himself back into reality. "Now the dry weather is making it throw off squares."

"Strike up a tune—'Grey Eagle'!"

"Sure." Bert launched into a bar. Some of the warmth sweeping through his veins must surely have reached into his fingers, for they needed no limbering up. They flew across the strings with a compelling, fluid motion. They set feet—even old Aunt Blanche's feet—to patting. They swirled over the notes like water pouring down the river in a rise.

"If I could play like that," Joyce sighed, "I would be perfectly happy. But haven't you ever made up any tune of your own?"

"I have," he confided in a low voice. "But I've run into trouble. There's no ending for it."

She leaned forward and clasped her hands together. "I don't care. Play it for me. Play me something different. Please do."

He considered. "I couldn't do that."

"And why not—if I ask you to?"

He was silent a moment. "After a while," he promised gently. "If you really want it, I will play it after a while. But just let me play the regular ones now."

So his bow moved like a satin ribbon, and his fingers like cotton leaves in a west wind. He ran through "Dusty Miller," "Billy in the Low Ground," "Forked Deer," "Texas Star," "Leather Breeches," and "The Eighth of January." Then he swung into "Mockingbird," and "Silver Bells." Finally, the tantalizing smell of cookies and cocoa in the kitchen began to penetrate through the maze.

"Let me choose you some cookies." Joyce reached into a pan and drew out raisin-studded squares. She slipped them into Bert's hand. A dimple danced at one corner of her red lips. "Don't you like what I gave you?"

He nodded mutely. He stood up. There was something he wanted to ask her, and he felt sure she would answer yes. Any girl who looked at a person the way she did him would be glad to ride home with him from a musicale.

Crockett crunched on a cookie and yawned again. His eyes were the color of a norther in spring. "There was a good show in town tonight."

"I don't like shows," Joyce answered. "I don't even like town."

"You would be an inexpensive person to keep around all the time," Crockett observed.

The crowd scattered toward the porch. Bert put his cookies in one pocket and moved to a solitary corner. He watched Joyce from a distance. Boys ebbed back and forth around her.

When the music began once more in the house, it was noticeable how Joyce managed to get back to the same chair. It took a bit of figuring, but there she sat again. Bert had to turn his head away to keep his mind on "Coming Down the Pecos," and "Sally Good'in."

Suddenly Joyce leaned forward and tossed her gleaming hair back down her shoulders. "Bert, you're stalling. I want you to play me that piece of your own."

"But I told you that I can't finish it."

"Never mind. I want to hear it."

He met her intent gaze. So she kept asking for it. Other fellows could sing songs and spiel sweet talk and drive long, oil-bought cars, and look like some fellow out of a book. But he could still play the fiddle. "All right."

"What's the name of this one now?"

"That's my secret." The other people in the room, their eyes fastened upon him, dissolved and faded away. There was only Joyce leaning forward in the chair, with that special smile flitting about her lips.

He felt the old hunger for fiddlestrings seize him. He wanted them to tell of the quicksilver play of emotion across her face, of the deep light resting in her eyes. He caressed the strings gently, and the sound was as sweet as mesquite honey. The guitars, groping, searched for a chord while Joyce moved across the wild notes with her hair blowing in the wind. She reached a hand for him from the tattered fog of a dream, and threw back her laughing face. He could see the quick beat of a pulse in the hollow of her throat. She led him to the edge of a hill, and looked into the morning beside him.

The strings kept on singing. Bert had completely confused all the guitar players, but that didn't matter. There was the gay trill of Joyce's laughter, and the heady warmth of her smile. Now came the time in the music when he reached to hold her—

Bert abruptly took his bow away from the strings. The room became still as a church, and then a hesitant and puzzled clapping echoed across it.

The crowd arose. "Are you through?" There were mutters. "Don't tell me it ends right there? Is this some kind of joke?"

Joyce stared at him. Some of the mist from the dream still clung to her eyes. "Is there no more?"

"No more now." He laid his violin in its case.

"But there has to be! There has to be some sort of—peace—to end such a song!"

"Maybe there will be, someday." He spoke to her evenly. He turned to the crowd. "If I'm to make a living farming cotton," he stated flatly, "I'd better go home and get some sleep."

Some of them laughed. "But Bert—you're always the last person to leave a musicale."

"That's all I can play tonight."

Joyce rose shakily from her chair. Bert turned to her, but at that instant old Aunt Blanche edged up and wedged in between them. She wanted to tell him how poorly she had felt lately, and with all those black-eyed peas to can, too. Her first man, she explained, had liked black-eyed peas cooked with fat pods of okra on top.

Bert vacantly muttered something and broke away from her. He walked toward the door with his fiddle case. But Joyce was gone. People were loading in the cars—gay, scuffling youngsters, and sleepy old folk. Where was she? He didn't like this feeling —something like strings being tuned higher and higher.

Then he saw her. She was standing in the checkered shadow of a big, twisted old mesquite tree on the south side of the yard. When he moved down the swaying steps she lifted her head and spoke.

"Bert—I've been waiting for you," she said.

He walked nearer, cautiously putting his case on the ground. "For me?" he asked through a tight throat.

"I have something to ask you. Look—" She turned her face toward the light. "Look how that feather of a cloud is going across the moon! Have you ever seen such a lovely night?"

"Never," he answered.

"I wish you would capture moonlight on that violin of yours. Every time I see a pretty thing I want to keep it always. Isn't there any way to capture something pretty and keep it forever?"

"I try," he said thickly. "I try."

She put one soft hand on his arm. "There is no one like you. Your music has—" Her voice wavered off into a tremolo. "But you can tell why I've been coming to so many Pecan Creek musicales. I don't need to go over all that with you—"

He stood mute and transfixed before the tree.

"But I'm taking up a lot of your time," she continued. "I simply wanted to ask you something. Would you be willing to play—for my wedding?"

Bert had known what it was like to have the *A* string snap while he was playing, but he had never known before what it was like to have *E* and *D* break too, and the whole bow collapse. There was no sound left.

"This is a secret, a real secret," Joyce breathed. "You see, Crockett's family doesn't like me very much. They think my folk are poor—and shiftless. So this is going to be just a little wedding. But I wanted some—music. And when I heard that piece of your own tonight, I knew what kind I wanted. So if you could be good enough—"

Bert searched for his voice again.

"I know this is quite a surprise. I'm so lucky. Isn't he handsome?"

"Joyce!" Crockett called from his car. Bert looked toward him. A sleek, oil-bought boat of a car—the clearly defined, arrogant features of the driver—the expensive fringed leather jacket— "I'm getting tired sitting here with this fool moonlight in my eyes!"

"Don't call it a fool moon!" Joyce chided. "It's a wonderful moon!" She smiled, and a bar of light broke across the branches and illuminated her face. Bert faltered before the radiance. He bowed his head again.

"Or maybe you don't *like* weddings," Joyce added slowly. "When I started coming over here, people warned me you were not interested in women. Maybe it's best. You might marry and forget your music. Married people sometimes do."

It was fortunate that he had learned to play on the bass string alone. Now he could go down the fingerboard and make a recognizable tone. "The way I feel about weddings is—they make me happy if the people being married are happy. I will play."

"Come over to the car for a moment." She led him forward. "Crockett, he will play for us!"

"Women!" Crockett shook his head. "They always want music and stuff! And do you know, Bert, what this Joyce wanted me to do tonight? Stop the car down where the road crosses Pecan Creek! And when I stopped it all she wanted to do was look at the water. She asked me to be quiet, said she wanted to listen to something she called 'night sounds'!"

"The tiny things in the button willows," Joyce interrupted. "There were funny little insects all beside the water, and they were singing tones to the moon. The moon had just touched the water. It was the most peaceful place—"

"Did you say 'peaceful'?" Bert whispered.

"Peaceful." She turned to him. "Oh, Bert—we must go now. But I will let you know the day of our wedding. And please make an ending to your music. I know you can."

Crockett spun the starter on the car. "I've got to get home. We're pouring kerosene on the home-pasture mesquite tomorrow morning."

"Oh, no!" Joyce burst out. "I like mesquite bloom! We'll see about that mesquite killing when I have a say in the matter!"

Crockett's young mouth curled. "I'll bet. Try to tell my dad that!"

Bert looked across at him. "Don't laugh, boy. You might be surprised someday at what you would do for her!"

They both laughed merrily. They sped away while Bert groped to his own car. It could still run. It could follow them—at a distance—down the dark shroud of a road toward the creek.

The motor died at the low-water crossing. Bert pulled over to one side of the road. He sat quietly under the wheel for a long while, until the mood had fallen toward the west.

The world had come out from under a shadow, and was silvering over again. The moon floated on the breast of the water— just as she had said.

There was a song moving down the whole creek. It was a quiet, gentle song—sort of a hushed lullaby. It murmured through the pecan grove and curled around the creamy bloom of the button willow. It ebbed through the throats of endless sleepy wild things.

Bert listened carefully. Then he pushed the car door open, picked up his violin, and stepped softly out into the night.

Autumn Episode

Upon the first frosty moments past sunrise Roy Martin heard a whistling near his front porch. The liquid, melodious quality of the sound told him that it belonged to Manuel Greigas, the most engaging of his flock of Mexican-national cotton pickers.

He pushed back the front door. "Come in, Manuel."

"Oh no, Señor. I will not bother your house. I stand outside."

"Nonsense." Roy kicked back the screen. "Boy, can't I get it through your head that you're in Texas now? You aren't supposed to stand on porches in the cold with your hat in your hand! Nor do you bow down and keep your eyes on the floor."

Manuel laughed, and fixed his bright black eyes upon Roy's face with a look of complete devotion.

"You are a good hombre, Señor," he said.

Roy hastily thought back through the weeks to the day when this group of nationals had waited for him in the Labor Camp at Big Spring. That lavender-and-gold September day hadn't veiled the starkness of their appearance; they had been hungry, ragged, tired, with a stoical facelessness which made each one look exactly like the other one. All except one—a certain fellow who had managed to salvage a bit of dash and gaiety. He had stepped forward to identify himself in shredded English as one Manuel Greigas. He was to be, he had announced proudly, the interpreter. Since then Manuel had followed Roy with the deftness of a willing shadow. His eyes tried to anticipate when Roy wanted a gate opened, or where he wanted the big cotton trailer moved.

"Have a seat on the couch," Roy offered. "You ready to ride into town?"

"All are ready, Señor. But I have something to ask you. I want to ask you more of that—Christmas—which you say will soon come. I never have one before. I do not want to have one," he twisted the words into a bubbling sound, "unless my people at home can have one too."

"That's easy, Manuel." Roy sat down beside him. "Look, you can buy a nice gift for your *señorita,* and a few for your best friends. Get the clerks in the store to wrap them fancy for you, and then put brown paper on the outside so you can mail them. Didn't you say you taught yourself to write? Then you can address them out correctly."

The glow faded from Manuel's eyes. "But, Señor, I cannot buy gifts for all I know in my town."

"Of course not. But you can fill in with Christmas cards for the rest of your friends."

"Cards?"

"Yes, Manuel. Greeting cards with pretty pictures. I'll show you what they are when we get to town. You can go tell the fellows I'm ready to go now."

Roy backed the red cotton truck out beside the barracks, and watched nationals scramble out. Manuel kept hanging back.

Roy turned to him. "Get up here with me, if you want to."

A smile spread across his whole face and he leaped into the cab of the truck.

"There's sure a lot of difference between the looks of these fellows now and when they came, isn't there, Manuel?"

"Oh, *sí!* When we come to you we wear shoes made of tires. The wind—he sing through our clothes. We all hungry. Now we warm, we fed."

They sped over the low hills to the valley holding the county seat. The little town lay under a haze of gin smoke and burning leaves. Roy parked the truck under some bright spangles on Main Street. Manuel hopped out and addressed the men in fluid Spanish punctuated with many gestures. He informed the hombres that he had much business to do, and that they must find their own way about the stores. When the sun reached so high they must be at the truck.

"Manuel," Roy asked, "don't you want me to help you find those Christmas cards? You may speak English, but you're not supposed to read the stuff."

Manuel shrugged. "Oh, Señor, you do not know me! I learn to read English now! I find my own things!"

Roy looked at him carefully. "You'd better take me up on my offer."

"No worry, Señor, no worry. I no have the trouble."

"All right, but you be sure and ask the clerk to show you the counter where the Christmas cards are."

It was before noon when Roy made his way back to the truck. Nationals were sitting around it eating rolls and Mexican sausages. Manuel was racing down the street. He was panting and radiant of expression.

"Señor!" he called.

As he came nearer, Ray saw that he was carrying a square package. He thrust it forward.

"Oh, Señor—merry the Christmas! But you no open now. You save for your Santa Claus stocking tree."

Roy found some words.

"Why, Manuel, you shouldn't have done this. But thank you —thank you very much. And I will save it. I won't open it now."

"You wait," Manuel repeated happily. I mail my other gifts.

I mail out lots of cards. I ask the lady to show me where are the Christmas cards. She tell me, and I find a long table with many cards. Some have pretty babies, some have horses, some have trees. I get the finest one of all. I make her get a box with all the same one, so my friends will no be the jealous. I get you the same kind too. You can see it now."

He proudly presented Roy with a square white envelope.

"It have many pretty flowers in it."

Roy's expression became puzzled. He slowly pulled a folder out of the envelope. Flowers—yes! Back came another flap. Inside was a picture of a beautiful brunette reclining upon a white bed. But it was the words which captured Roy's startled gaze. They began—SO GLAD YOUR OPERATION WAS A SUCCESS—

Roy sucked in a desperate breath. He glanced at the eager, spellbound face. He placed the card carefully in his pocket.

"Manuel, you are a wonder," he said. "This is the prettiest Christmas card anyone ever gave me!"

Little Oil Stove

The tall Negro straightened over a row of frost-blackened cotton. "Fletch," he called back down the row, "you ready to weigh up?"

Fletch looked up. A smile flashed across his broad black face. "I shore am, Clay." He tugged at his sack. "I shore will be glad to quit. I've had a crick in my back ever since mornin'."

Clay swung his long cottonsack over his back. The men were almost the same size, tall, broad of shoulder. But instead of Fletch's wide and friendly face, flashing a variety of expressions, Clay had features which were straight and strangely reserved.

They walked heavily toward the scales. "Look there in the north," Fletch grunted. "Looks like that norther is blowin' in fast. I seen it first right after dinner; jist a little blue streak low down. I shore hope it don't git cole. I ain't got much beddin' along. Mebbe I could talk the Parson out of a quilt."

"Is that broken-down oil stove the only heater we have in the shack?" asked Clay.

"Yep," Fletch answered. "Besides our cookstove, of course. It wouldn't give much heat." He let his cottonsack drop in front of the mesquite poles holding up the cotton scales. His faded blue shirt ripped across the muscles of his back. "Boy," he chuckled, "that norther's gonna feel cole when it starts whistlin' through this shirt. Lissen, I been savin' my money this fall; I ain't bought me no clothes. I been stayin' outa town, 'way from dice games an' wil' wimmin. I aim to buy me a little truck patch some of these days, back in East Texas. How come you didn't go to town with the rest of the pickers this evenin'?"

"Me?" Clay picked up a jar of water, and took several gulps. "Me? I'd better stay out of town too. I've just finished doing time down in Shawnee County for knocking down a white man."

Fletch's eyes widened. "What was th' trouble?"

"He tried to beat me out of my hoeing money."

"Well, that's somethin' we don't hafta worry 'bout here," Fletch answered quickly. "We got a good boss here. Why Mista Ashley went and had these scales tested so he'd be shore an' not cheat us on our weights."

Clay turned around. "Good Mr. Ashley," he said evenly. "I'll bet he stays awake nights, worrying about us."

Soon both sacks were weighed and pulled away from the scales. "Let's rest 'fore we empty," Fletch suggested. He sat heavily down on his sack. "You got a cigarette paper?"

Clay sat down and fished one out of his pocket.

"Lissen," Fletch continued as he rolled his cigarette, "I been wantin' to talk to you, Clay. Ever since th' day you walked up to th' field askin' for a job, I've had a funny likin' for you. You could be a right kind of feller." He took a long drag from his cigarette. "And th' funny thing is, you talk like a feller who has a good education. Now me—I'm jist a field Nigger. But you— you could be somthin' diff'rent. Why you travelin' 'round, pickin' cotton? You could git a better job."

"A job doing what?" Clay slowly asked. "Being a porter on a train? Cleaning up the operating room of some white man's hospital?"

Fletch shook his head. "Boy, you got a chip on yore shoulder a mile wide. Lissen, Clay, I've knowed people of all kinds. I seen good white men, and bad ones. I seen good Niggers, and bad ones."

They became silent. Across the northern horizon a dark blue

smudge was rising. In front of it was a line of red dust. A chill was gathering over the gaunt cottonstalks.

"We better empty and tromp our cotton 'fore that whistler catches us." Fletch jumped up and swung over the trailer endgates. He pulled up Clay's sack.

Dust started whirling down the cotton rows before they packed the cotton. "Jist a little more trompin'," urged Fletch. "This win's strong 'nough to blow Mista Ashley's cotton right outa the trailer."

Clay shrugged. Finally Fletch tucked the empty sacks carefully around the cotton. "This win's shore cole." He shivered as he climbed down from the trailer. "Got yore kneepads? Let's beat it to th' shack."

Beyond the field, past a barbed-wire fence and a mesquite thicket, stood an old house. The wind sang across the rotted sagging roof and through a broken window light. Fletch and Clay jumped the fence, and dodged a chaparral bush.

The warped front door was blown open. "Lemme in," panted Fletch. "I left a stewer of beans open. That sand'll cover 'em up."

Clay followed behind and pulled the door shut. "Hand me that chair." He grabbed the only chair in the room—a scarred cane-bottomed one—and propped it against the doorknob. "That wind is like ice. Throw me that old sack over there."

"You know," Fletch remarked as he threw the sack, "you an' me was lucky gettin' good corners to sleep in. When the Parson was dividin' out corners for us pickers I was 'fraid I was gonna end up by that broke winder. Look, I got room outa th' win' here for my pallet an' two apple boxes."

"Hand me that blame rusty little stove. Has the thing any coal oil in it?" Clay began to shake the flimsy oil heater. He put a match to the wick and watched a feeble flame struggle upward.

"Shore hope that thing heats the house," whispered Fletch.

"Of course it can't heat the house," Clay said. "A shack like this? Why can't a man fix his workers a decent place to live?"

"Well now—" soothed Fletch, "I like a good place to live as well as anybody. Someday I'm gonna own me a little white-painted house. I'm gonna have water piped inside, an' a real bathroom. But till then, I don' blame Mista Ashley much. The Ashleys is plain folks. Look at his house over there 'cross that ridge. You kin tell that it's jist a plain house."

"Sure. But you said one time that he has good butane stoves."

"You oughta see what some farmers in this country lives in," Fletch evaded. "Big fine houses, with pickers in henhouses. I'm proud we got a pickerhouse this good. It don' do no good to build a fine house for pickers. Look what Lonnie Johnson's done drawed on this wall. The Parson was shore mad when he seen those pictures."

"You always take up for Ashley, don't you?" broke in Clay. "All right, bow and scrape all you want to."

"Let's forgit it and git somethin' to eat," suggested Fletch in a dull voice.

As the men ate, the oil heater began to smoke more and more. "That stove!" Clay put down his tin plate. "I ought to throw it out the door."

"Oh, don' do that," Fletch said quickly. "Mista Ashley put it out here. It's his heater."

"I ought to ram it down his throat. There he sits over in his warm house, surrounded with land he didn't earn, in front of a big butane fire."

"Well, we kin crawl in our pallets, when we finish eatin'."

"Drat a smoking heater." Clay turned it out.

"Mebbe it won' git too cole t'night."

"It's already too cold."

Fletch spooned down the last of his beans. "I'll git th' Parson to see Mista Ashley first thin' in th' mornin', 'fore th' Ashleys leave for church. He'll git this oil stove fixed."

"In the morning?" Clay turned around. "Are you crazy? *I'm* going over to see Mr. Ashley right now, myself. When *I* get through with him he'll be glad to put a butane stove out here. If he's able, that is!"

"Clay, don' joke." Fletch frowned. "You know th' Parson's th' head of us bunch of pickers. He allus does th' business with Mista Ashley."

Under Clay's chiseled features there came a faint grayish cast. "Don't try to stop me. I'm going to see Mr. Ashley."

"Now, Clay, lissen!" Fletch grabbed his arm. "Don' you go over there to Mista Ashley's house! I'm 'fraid you migh' git to arguin', lose yore head, an' make trouble. You say you already been in trouble—you cain't 'ford no more trouble with a white man."

"Is that so?" Clay's lips curled. "It'll be worth plenty to tell Mr. Ashley what I think of him and his land and his stoves." He jerked away from Fletch's arm, and walked out the door into the norther. When he slammed the door it swayed back to show him a last glimpse of Fletch's bewildered face.

He walked silently down a low valley which separated the pickers' house from Mr. Ashley's white bungalow. A bone-chilling blast of wind howled through the gray catclaw. He shivered and bowed his head.

Suddenly he lurched forward, stumbling. He pulled himself upright, and discovered that he had stepped off the side of the hill into some kind of a cellar. It was almost overgrown with broomweeds.

He looked about curiously. Had someone once lived here? It was small, not nearly so large as one of the rooms of the pickers' house. The whole thing had a weathered look, as if it was quite old. There were stacks of flat gray rocks around the sides, possibly once supports of some sort of roof.

Against one side of the dirt wall a flat slab was propped. There was something carved upon it. Clay read the words slowly.

JOHN AND PHOEBE ASHLEY
SETTLED 1882

He stared at it. The words burned into his eyes. He sat down on the cold ground and ran his fingers over the smooth surface of the rock and across the grooves a knife had made long ago.

Moments passed. He no longer felt the wind.

"Boy, where are you?" Fletch's voice, torn by the wind, echoed from the hillside above him. "Am I gonna hafta trail you all th' way to Mista Ashley's?" He stared. "What you doin', sittin' here in this ole caved-in dugout? It's coler'n th' pickers' house."

"I just—stepped into it before I knew. Come on down. I didn't know it was here."

"You been to Mista Ashley's yet?"

"No."

"Thank th' Lord! This dugout? Mista Ashley showed it to me one day. This is what his grandad lived in when he first come to West Texas. That's his grandad and grandma's name, cut there on th' rock." He huddled down. "When they come here this country was pretty wile. They had lots of hard times; you oughta git Mista Ashley to tell you 'bout it sometime. Say, that's who Mista Ashley got his lan' from."

"You never did mention this before," Clay said.

"Boy—are you outa yore mine?" Fletch laughed. "Me mention

somethin' good 'bout Mista Ashley's fam'ly to you? You'd think I was takin' up for 'im."

Clay smiled thinly. "Then his grandparents homesteaded this land?"

"Shore they did. Come out here in a covered wagon. Come in when the buffalo hunters did. And Mista Ashley tole me he was prouder of this ole dugout an' rock slab than anythin' else on th' farm. He said it showed the Ashleys was willin' to earn what they got." Fletch leaned against the side of the dugout. "Say, it's warmer here, outa th' win'. Guess that's why they build a dugout —'cause they didn't have no fancy stoves to keep warm with. You know—I was thinkin' one day. My folks niver left me no lan' nowheres. My Grandad and Grandma Runnels niver cut their names on no rock slabs. They could've, jist th' same's th' Ashleys. They was free, back in 'eighty. They could've come out here." He grinned. "I reckin they was too busy seein' if they could beat some white man back in Alabama outa some corn an' black-eyed peas."

Clay looked silently about.

"But you take me," Fletch said half aloud, "I'm gonna have me a little truck patch back in East Texas some of these days. I'm gonna have a white-painted house, with water piped inside. Then I'm gonna find a rock, an' cut my name on it. An' jist let somebody try t' take it away from my grandkids!"

Clay's hands were clasping and unclasping.

"Boy, let's git to a warm place!" Fletch jumped up. "Grandad Ashley kin have his dugout back. Me, I'm headed to th' shack." He looked closely at Clay. "You niver heared a word I said. Let's go back. Don' go git in trouble with th' Ashleys. The Parson'll be in 'fore dark. He kin figger out somethin' to do 'bout that stove."

"The stove?" Clay stood up. "I was just sitting here thinking about it. That butane business I was talking about—just forget it. You know, there's a good stand of mesquite along this hill. Some look half dead. They ought to burn. Isn't there an old *wood* heater thrown away behind the picker house?"

"Shore. An' there's not much wrong with it. 'Cept nobody wan's to cut wood."

"Then I'll go borrow an axe, and we'll cut some wood."

"But Clay—" Fletch broke in, "Mista Ashley says cotton pickers won' cut wood no more. He says they'd druther freeze 'round a oil heater."

"But he might be wrong." Clay smiled. "Sometimes a man can be—wrong."

The Red Geranium

When I thought of the Miles family before that March morning, it was with vague superiority. They were new to our Southwestern community, having recently rented a river farm consisting of sandy, scrub-oak thickets—an unhappy contrast to the more fertile land around my home. And if my girlish life at seventeen sometimes seemed bleak, at least I was spared the elemental struggles of such families.

My mother was bending over a geranium growing under our living-room window. Its large flower had blossomed in a vivid color—rosy scarlet, with an iridescent glow. Mother raised beautiful house plants, but this was the most striking she had ever grown.

"Why can't something exciting happen?" I asked. "Even a funeral would be better than having nowhere to go."

Mother's startled gaze followed me out the door, where peach blossoms spilled hesitant fragrance. Suddenly a car stopped in front of our house. The driver spoke to Mother and hurriedly left.

"Bad news from the Miles family," she explained sadly. "Their week-old baby girl died last night."

I shrugged. "They are probably better off. They still have seven children left."

Mother evaded my remark. "We should go over there, but we don't have the car today. Would you walk?"

"Me? Why?"

"Because I ask you to. I would like you to take a flower."

"A flower? But we have nothing to give but peach blooms, and those seem kind of out of place for a funeral."

Then I realized where Mother's gaze was traveling. She picked up scissors and started toward the red geranium.

"No!" I protested. "You can't send it. It's the loveliest flower anywhere around. You've cared for the thing all winter. You'll never have such a flower again."

Mother quickly clipped the stem beneath the bloom. While I watched in stunned silence, she surrounded it with asparagus fern and decorated the spray with a white bow.

"I suppose I might as well take it," I sighed, "but it seems such a waste."

With the flower in a shoe box I walked north and cut cross country. Beyond the river the Miles house crouched against a sand dune. Inside the kitchen neighbors greeted me quietly. A daughter, Esther, smiled. Her clothing, although old, was neat. The house, I noticed, was also spotlessly clean.

"I have a flower here." I handed her the box.

She lifted the lid quickly, and was so moved that she could scarcely answer. "It's so nice of you to bring it. You see, this is the only flower we have."

I was shocked. Not that were were used to lavish funeral displays, but there had always been wreaths.

"Let's show Mother."

Hesitantly I followed her in where a pale, worn woman lay in bed. A tear glistened on one of her cheeks, but she tried to smile at me.

"Look, Mother—she brought a flower for the baby."

When Mrs. Miles opened the box, some of the glow from the flower seemed to light her face. She touched the bloom gently, as if it were a sacred thing. "How lovely. I was hoping that my baby would have at least one flower."

I felt tears spring into my eyes. This was a new insight into mother love. What a strange thing—it could be divided without diminishing!

"Would you like to see the baby?" Esther asked.

We entered a room where there was a sheet-covered bench. Diffused light touched the simple little casket resting upon it. The baby had the look of a translucent china doll. She was fine of feature, with a wide brow. She might have done great things —she might have—

I moved away. Inside the kitchen I tried to make conversation with the women preparing food. But I could no longer be casual about the Miles baby. She had become a personality to me, not just an unknown creature gone to an ageless sleep. The mystery of life and death seemed shrouded in that small, fragile frame.

At midafternoon our little group stood quietly in the community cemetery. Heavy veils of cloud darkened the sun. The wind was rising; it fluttered the pages of the Bible in the minister's hands and whistled across the tiny grave before us.

Had I stayed away from the Miles family, I reflected, it might have been easy to remain indifferent to their troubles. But here I was beside them, with tears to match their own.

I glanced toward the wooden cross marking the grave. The red geranium lay at its feet, with petals beginning to shrivel and blacken. How drab our living room must look without the bright bloom! But suddenly I understood, along with my mother, that one flower was a small price to pay for teaching her daughter compassion.

Talisman

As young Ben Decker rode beside Sam Wybolt in the front seat of the old car late that December day, he could hear Sam's voice droning along like wild bees hunting a cave to swarm in. But Sam was not too worrisome; Ben could think his own thoughts and catch back up with the conversation without any trouble. At least another day was over and he was out of the cotton patch—gone from the rasping stalks and heavy sacks. Maybe, as time went by, he could even unthread some of the maze in his own mind. For he had fallen into the habit, even before he started drifting across Western Texas, of expecting nothing good to come to him outside of his own efforts. And it would take a while to mull over this sudden stroke of luck, which promised him a job with Old Ellis Morgan. A chance—if things worked out right—to slip some extra money beside that hidden in his own bedroll.

He buttoned the collar of his worn denim jacket tighter against the biting air, and pulled his black hat over his ears. A norther was swinging in on West Texas. Already the river, leading from cotton farms to ranch country, was shadowy with cold. "I'll bet it sure will be icy in the morning," Sam was saying. "Look at them ducks hurrying ahead of that dirty roll of cloud. We'll catch some sand before we get to the Old Man's ranch house. Like I was saying, boy, I'm glad to help you get a better job from Old Ellis Morgan—"

Ellis Morgan. That name again. Ben's cool blue eyes flicked

with a sudden electric spark, like pieces of flint nicked by steel. There was a magic sound to that name; a fascination shrouding the rich, tottering old rancher who bore it. There was a story behind the name which anyone who cared a thing about the history of the region had heard, even a stray cotton picker such as Ben. For Ellis Morgan and the white buffalo he had killed were part of the legend and folklore of the Upper Colorado watershed. When he made trips into the county-seat town, men cleared a little path for him down the street and opened doors ahead. For he had been an Indian scout and an explorer, a famous buffalo hunter, and the first white man to settle the territory. His vitality had propelled him far beyond his era—into an age where he saw fat Herefords grazing and oil wells chugging across his sprawling empire. Ben had never expected even to see the man, much less get a chance to work for him.

Sam's voice edged in. "It was pure luck that I happened to run into the Old Man in town—right after I heard in the cafe that he needed a boy to help him out. It was a cold day for him to be stirring; he's ninety years old. But I guess he doesn't trust anyone else to do his business. Now don't misunderstand me— he's a decent man and he'll treat you right. But he's very odd about many things, and especially money. He doesn't even trust banks very far; I've heard that most of his cash is in a special box in a safe there in his ranch house. And he doesn't trust anyone else with the safe combination—you can be sure of that! I've heard that even his foreman doesn't know how to open it."

Ben moistened his tongue.

"So I thought of you right then," Sam continued, "and knew you should have a chance at something better. So I chased the old fellow down—I've known him since I was a kid. I told him that one of the finest boys I had ever seen has been picking cotton for me all fall and sleeping in my barn. He got interested right away and wanted to know where you came from and what you were doing in this country."

Ben's gaze narrowed slightly above the high planes of his cheeks.

Sam slowed the car. "Look over there—did you see that coyote run behind that chaparral? There must be a dead cow somewhere close; I'll tell Old Ellis to have his foreman send out one of the boys tomorrow. I told him—" Sam shifted his numbed hands on the steering wheel, "that I didn't know all the story, but that your parents died when you were young, and an uncle back in Lone Star County hadn't watched after your farm well enough to keep it from being foreclosed. You'd lived around with different kinfolk, got disgusted at crowding in, and decided to drift out here. Too many older fellows were out of work, so you couldn't get a ranch job.

"Well, after that speech of mine, I believe the old fellow would've hired you sight unseen, if it hadn't been for another funny notion of his. He thinks he can tell all about a person by looking him straight in the eyes, and he won't trust anyone to work on his ranch before he looks at him and talks to him. Even his foreman can't hire a hand without letting the old fellow peer into his eyes. Now of course you won't be under the foreman. You'll be right with the Old Man all the time, and whatever he has you doing will be a sight easier than chasing down scrap cotton."

No doubt about it, Ben thought, Old Ellis Morgan had picked the cream of the country for his ranch. When they passed through his plank gate the turf grew thicker across the pastures. Occasional clumps of mesquite dotted undulating rises. The road to the headquarters made Ben catch his breath in sudden admiration. It spiraled gently into the sunset—toward a fresh-water creek lined with hackberry, pecan, and willow. On a rise beyond, the road circled heavy old mesquites to where a ranch house punctuated the horizon.

"He built this thing years ago, after he married." Sam waved his arm wide enough to include the towering gray walls, and a cluster of corrals, barns, and sheds. "The house is three stories high, and a fancy thing inside. Windows all over the place. Someone said Ellis tried to pattern it after mansions where he came from—back in New England. He had those cement blocks specially made and hauled in by wagon, and woodwork and marble and tile sent from everywhere under the sun. He ordered silver from Mexico, china from England, furniture from New York City. And that safe—there's no telling where he sent to for that!"

Ben looked thoughtfully at the icy water underneath the little bridge they were crossing.

"Once the house was built, I don't think all of it was used very often. People living around here weren't invited to visit the Morgans much. Just business friends from Fort Worth, or the oil company which drilled on the land. Then Ellis' wife died, and there wasn't much of anyone."

A patch of lawn surrounded the house, with a few trees, but no amount of shrubbery could have softened its vast, stark outlines.

"Now come on, boy. The Old Man is waiting to see you."

Ben followed Sam past the clanging iron gate, past a shivering Mexican trying to tie a blanket around an oleander bush. They rang a bell on the porch, and a Negro cook opened the door. Ben slipped past the magnificence of carpets, chandeliers, and rosewood furniture. The trail circled tile-and-brass fireplaces, varnished doors with silver knobs, and mirrors and carved stair-cases. Finally they reached a glassed-in sunroom where cow horns decorated one wall and leather-covered chairs were scattered about. A slender figure rose. Ben realized that the man was older than anyone he had ever seen, and that only his eyes seemed really alive. The rest of him was weathered and shrunken, like an old hide which had hung too long across the corral fence.

Ellis Morgan was not a large man, but as he moved he drew himself upward in a gesture of command. Ben saw that his thatch of hair was still dark and well trimmed, and he had clean plain clothes and expensive boots. But it was his eyes which riveted Ben's uneasy attention—eyes as black and penetrating as those of an Indian. Lenslike, they seemed to probe into some dark recess of Ben's soul. He felt their ageless weighing.

Finally he saw the drawn lips move. "Sam, you had good judgment this time. He can stay." Old Ellis turned to Ben. "I have no one left who cares to stay with me—day and night. I have had a heart attack; I will have others. I need someone nearby with sense enough to give me the right tablets." His voice rippled with disgust. "I have seen people die during all my life. I tried to be clever, and outsmart outlaws and Indians. Now why can't I go like the rest—quickly and be done with it? But no— the doctor says something—and I listen to the doctor." He tapped his fingers on the arm of a chair. "Sit down. We will not be tied in the house all the time. You will drive me about the pastures, go to town, take trips to Fort Worth. You can read to me, learn how to keep my books and answer my letters. You will get twenty dollars each week."

"Yes, sir." Ben ran numb fingers through his soft black crown of hair.

"Let me show you your room. We'll stay here on the ground

floor; the upstairs is closed off now. There never was any use for it; don't know why I built it in the first place. You can go up and see the rooms if you please; there's a ballroom where we once had a reception for the governor. Oh—Sam Wybolt, thank you for your trouble."

"Nothing at all, sir." Sam fingered his hat respectfully. "Hope the boy works out for you."

Ben hesitated a moment, then lugged his little bundles around to the back door and through the kitchen. "Boy, have you eaten?" asked Ellis Morgan.

"Yes, sir."

"You will always find plenty in the kitchen. Still, it doesn't taste like campfire food." His voice edged away, and finally returned. "Your room—put your things in that room there." The old man reached for a cane, and led the way. "My room and yours join each other. You can hear me if I call in the night."

Ben stared at the spacious bedrooms, the soft beds, the heavy drapes framing the windows. There were bright Indian rugs laid on the floors, and mesquite fires in each fireplace. Ben tried not to stare at the paintings on the walls, all showing Indians, frontiersmen, buffaloes, and horses.

"Is this all right, boy? We will leave my door half open. There are books for you to read—paper and pen on the desk. Now let me show you about my medicine—"

Ben listened carefully. When the Old Man tottered back to his own room Ben sat uneasily on the edge of his bed and pulled his money box from one old quilt. He counted it carefully and replaced it. He wouldn't need his battered covers now, so he scooted them into the depths of the closet. His clothes made a lonesome little patch on hangers.

He glanced toward where the money box was hidden. Before,

there had been just a vague, painful gnawing inside him—he hadn't known exactly what to want. But now he knew—this house and ranch and power was what money could buy. He could add to his money—slowly, steadily. He could spend nothing, play up to the old man. And finally—he might even feel his fingers close around the door to the safe. Who would know the difference—in case something happened to the Old Man?

Any stirrings from Ellis Morgan's room were blotted out by the wind, which had risen with the darkness. Its icy fingers probed for crevices in the stout old house. Ben settled slowly against the luxury of his bed.

"Boy—" called Ellis Morgan, "you don't have to go to bed so soon. Will you come see about this window, please?"

Ben found Ellis sitting like a night-shirted dummy in a chair by the fire. He pulled the window down against the shriek of the wind. "Boy—" Ellis asked suddenly, "do you like your bed?"

"Why yes, sir. I have never seen a bed like it. It is fine, and soft—"

"So I once said," Ellis answered dryly. He poked at a blazing mesquite stump. "My beds are far too soft." The fire cast long shadows across his face, and gleamed in his eyes. "Sit down."

"Yes, sir."

"The time has finally come—" Ellis cleared his throat—"when I have to hire someone to listen to me. No one else has time—no one else cares. But you are being paid, so you will listen."

Ben met his deep gaze.

Ellis Morgan's voice became an incantation. "If you could have seen this country as I saw it that morning, long before cotton farmers ruined it, with April on the hills, and a soft, sweet breeze rising from the south! I had been hunting buffalo for several years, sometimes on the outskirts of Comanche camps. I was an orphan, and I had been a drifter until I got into the business of buffalo hides. Then, in Comanche camps to the east, I kept hearing how fine and fat the buffalo were up the creek with the deep-blue water. There was a story—an Indian legend—of a sacred white buffalo who roamed in this area. If a man found this buffalo, great fortune would be his.

"So I came riding into this country, looking about. I found no Indians—they had drifted to the plains—but plenty of buffalo signs. And the creek—this pretty little fresh-water creek—gave me cool drinks and game and firewood all the way. One morning I crested the rise east of where the house is here, and met a sight I will never forget. A valley spread back from the creek—carpeted with fine grass and bright flowers. An in the middle of the flowers stood the white buffalo, with its hide gleaming silver in the sun.

"I was a hunter, a killer I suppose, so I shot the buffalo. I took the shining hide and stretched it out to dry. Then I looked about and knew my roaming days were over. I was more Comanche than I had realized; I would never leave this valley where my fortune lay."

Ben sat quietly, watching the faded lips move. A fire chunk snapped, sending sparks hissing against the wind. "Sounds like it's sleeting. Did you know that an Indian tepee made of hide would be warmer than this house tonight?"

"No, sir."

"I should have known this house wasn't worth any time and trouble." The Old Man pulled forward. "Enough of that. Bedtime. There's one more thing I would like for you to do. Step in the hall there, open the door across from it, go in the room with my safe, and open it up."

"Your safe, sir?" Ben moved visibly. "Me—open your safe?"

"Of course. Oh, I see you've been hearing stories the poor, ignorant cotton farmers tell about me. They probably told you I had silver dollars lined in rows on the walls. Anyone they can't understand—is speculated about. Go on—it isn't locked."

Ben rose slowly to his feet. "Are you sure—sir?" He moved gingerly across the room, pushed back the bedroom door, and soon walked into a room not much larger than his own closet. He looked at the knob of the safe.

"Go on—open it!" the Old Man called. "Bring me back what it has inside!"

Ben experimented with the knob, and reached inside. His fingers touched the heavy robe. He saw its aging silver gleam, felt its soft warmth envelop his hand.

"That's what I built the safe for in the first place," Ellis Morgan explained. "And tonight, with the wind whistling like in the old days, I want to sleep warm and comfortable. Unroll the white robe down by the bed here, where I can lie down and wrap up in it." His eyes searched Ben's face. "Well, boy—" he added, "my safe is empty. Do you have anything you'd like to leave in it? I should know that orphans carry little treasures around with them."

Ben drew a deep breath. "Nothing to compare with yours," he finally answered. "No—nothing. Nothing worth locking up— and planning a life around."

Letters

One bright April morning Lee Dawson braked his ranch pickup to a halt in front of the Hackberry Creek post office. He unfastened his spurs, gave the black horse riding in back a quick pat, and swung across the porch in his scuffed boots. Once inside the dim post office, he stepped eagerly to the line of closed mailboxes. He gave a deft twist to his own box, but his young face darkened when he drew out only a handful of thick circulars and unsealed advertisements.

"Silas,"—he spoke to the dried-up postmaster through the stamp window—"didn't I get a single personal letter this time?"

"Don't think so, Lee," the postmaster answered. "And your box looked so blamed empty I decided to fill it up with *something*, so I put in everything I had left over from the rural routes."

"Yeah, *something*," Lee agreed glumly. "Ads offering to come over here and drag off dead cattle free of charge to the glue factory. Burial insurance policies warning me that I better start making payments on my funeral. What do they think we are over here, anyway?"

Silas thought a moment, while Lee stared morosely at his mail. "Lee," he spoke slowly, "for a young fellow—and a nice young fellow at that—you're in a rut. Do you know what a rut is, boy? It's a grave with both ends knocked out! Don't you know anyone at all who will write you letters? Didn't you meet with anyone while you were in the Army? How come all these other boys around here brought back a pretty bunch of blonde-headed war brides, and you didn't bring home nobody?"

"You done forgot where I went during the war," Lee grinned feebly. "Out of boot camp and straight to New Guinea. I sure didn't see no blonde-headed women over there."

Silas shook his head. "Well, it's a pity. And you with one of the nicest little ranches in this part of Texas. Why, lots of girls would give plenty to catch a guy like you! You ought to take a trip into San Angelo; give yourself a chance to meet somebody."

"Aw, I couldn't do that." Lee wiped his forehead nervously. "I wouldn't know how to get acquainted with no girl."

"Boy, you don't hafta know! Just one look at you and one word about your ranch—and those San Angelo girls will do the rest! Listen, fellow, do you aim to sit on Rattlesnake Creek alone until you kill yourself with your own cooking? You take my advice— Say, I got a cousin in San Angelo—runs a big store down there. Knows everybody in town—his wife gives lots of nice parties for young folks. I'll give you his address. You drop by and get acquainted with him."

"Maybe you got something there, Silas." Lee's eyes lit up. "Maybe I *have* stayed at home too close. Things have got to a pretty pass when I can't get a letter from anybody on this earth."

The freshness of April gave way to the blasting heat of summer. Scorching July burned out into August and cool September. One gold-and-purple morning Silas was sorting mail in his same corner when Lee's pickup came to a familiar stop. But Lee's appearance had changed. He had a fresh haircut and starched clothing on. He swatted in irritation at his stiff shirt collar. And there was no horse in the back of the pickup any more. There were piles of rolled-up wallpaper and cans of paint.

"Howdy, Lee." Silas waved at him. "Wait a minute, and I'll

have your mail put up. Say, you sure do have a lot to thank me for. How's your wife? She like the ranch any better by now?"

"Some." Lee opened his mouth to say more, but decided to hush.

"Well, it *is* quite a bit different from town life." Silas tossed a letter aside. "Say, I hear she had a nice home in San Angelo."

"Sure did." Lee looked down at the floor.

"Well, it may seem lonesome to her out here for awhile, but she'll get used to it. She sure is a pretty girl. Dresses real nice, too."

"Yeah," Lee grunted.

"Well, here's your mail. No shortage for you any more, boy." Silas began to thumb through the stack of letters. "A letter from the new dry-goods store, a letter from the fanciest grocery in the county seat, one from a flower shop, a letter from a culture club, and a letter from some book-o'-the-month club. And here's a letter from the Hallmark Furniture Company from Fort Worth. What more c'd you want?"

Lee accepted the heap of letters, and glanced at them wearily. Then he stuffed them, unopened, into one shirt pocket.

"Well, so long, Silas." He started slowly toward the door.

"Wait a minute, boy!" Silas called to him. "That's not all your mail. Look here—here's a big C.O.D. package—come in just this morning. Says 'Sheet Music' on it."

Lee turned around. "Silas,"—he looked up wistfully— "sometimes, just for ol' times sake, couldn't you just stuff my box full of leftover ads like you used to do?"

Yellow-Headed Woman

On that afternoon Wesley Quitman stopped to talk to him, Cliff Allison was heading maize across a sandy West Texas hill. Cliff was following a black mule and a slide down between the green rows, chopping off the rust-colored maize heads with a pocketknife.

Wesley's Ford chugged to a stop over on the road across the strip of maize and cotton. Cliff drove the mule to the turnrow and looped the lines over a crooked mesquite post.

" 'Lo, Wes. Want a job?" Cliff laughed as Wesley walked up beside him.

Wesley was as tall as Cliff, but heavier. He was blond where Cliff was dark-haired, and he had a broader face. Instead of gray eyes, his were a rather bright blue. He had a wide mouth to match his wide hands and feet.

"Nuthin' doin'," he answered. "I got too much maize at home to head. Boy, I'm glad this-here cotton is openin', so I'll have a good excuse to get out of the maize patch. Cotton may drag you to death, but it sure won't make you itch!"

Cliff brushed off a clump of Colorado grass, and they sat down. The mule happily crunched on a maize head while Wesley turned to look at Cliff.

"Cliff," he burst out, "I got somethin' worryin' me; I might as well admit it." He picked up a maize head and began to make aimless marks in the red sand.

Cliff grinned. "I could guess what it is."

"How do you know?" Wesley asked quickly.

"What usually worries you? Annabelle Sessums."

Wesley grinned mournfully. "Yer right. But lissen, boy, this is jus' between me an' you an' that fence post over there. If some nosey ol' cuss like Essie Driggers was t' find out about this all of Red Bluff an' West Texas would soon know my troubles."

"Troubles?" Cliff asked. "I thought you an' Annabelle were goin' to get married."

"Like yer foot!" Wesley snorted. "Boy, I sometimes wish I'd never seen that gal!"

"Why don't you fergit her? There's better-lookin' girls here around Red Bluff. And did you ever look at Annabelle's mamma, Miz Sessums? Someday Annabelle will look jus' like her."

Wesley shook his head firmly. "No, she won't, Annabelle won't ever be that fat. Besides, look at that yellow hair of hers. I sure go for a yellow-headed woman. No, sir, I never could fergit that hair." He sighed. "But like I was sayin', Annabelle has sure got me up a tree. First she tole me she'd marry me this fall. Then she said she'd hafta have another room built on my house. Now she's gettin' fussy with me; jus' hard t' please."

"About what?" Cliff stretched and watched a lazy thunderhead floating overhead in the clear sky.

"Aw, about little things. Like th' other day—she'd bought a lot of records for her victrola. She made me sit an' lissen at 'em; when I said I didn't like 'Blue Yodel No. 2' she lit right into me. Said I didn't know how to 'preciate good music, an' I didn't have good manners. Said I wasn't romantic, neither."

"What does she call romantic?"

"I don't know," Wesley shook his head. "Personal, I figger I'm about th' best she can do. After all, I got a good sandy-land farm. Why that gal would be fixed for life—she never would hafta get out an' work in somebody else's cotton patch. So I reckon she'll go ahead an' marry me—after grumblin' awhile. But who wants a gal who's always lookin' for somethin' romantic t' come along?"

"I hope I don't never fall in love," Cliff laughed.

"You jus' wait. Let's see—yer nineteen now. Jus' give yerself another year or two. Boy, I bet when you fall, you fall like a ton o' bricks." He looked across the maize stalks, and a sudden expression of disgust crossed his face. "I jus' wish you would look. Speakin' of Essie Driggers—look at th' ole thing come steppin' across over here. He must have some bad news he's itchin' to tell."

" 'Lo, boys." Essie Driggers' lean brown shape ambled nearer. "Look at th' leaf worms in this cotton. If it wasn't September they'd eat it up. Jus' thought I'd stop by," he explained, stepping around the slide. "I come by Sessums jus'a few minutes ago."

Wesley's eyes kindled. "They all right?"

Essie grinned. "All right? I never seen 'em do better! I knowed if I didn't stop and tell you what I seen over there you'd be mad at me."

Wesley looked perplexed. "What'd you see?"

"Well, it was this-a-way." A satisfied look had come over Essie Driggers' sunburnt face. "I had t' go see Matt Sessums about a cotton trailer, an' on th' way t' his house I seen th' whole bunch in th' cotton patch. Then I noticed that two o' th' pickers was off t' theyselves. They was pickin' with their heads down, talkin' together. An' when one looked up—," he paused, "I saw it was that yeller-headed gal you claim, Annabelle."

There was no sound but the swishing of the mule's tail brushing away flies.

"An' th' other one," Essie finished, "was a dressed-up fine-lookin' young stranger."

"Aw, now—Essie!" scoffed Wesley. "You wouldn't hooraw a feller, would ya?"

"I'm not hoorawin' nobody," Essie declared. "You go see fer yerself."

"Well," Cliff smiled, "where'd he come from?"

"Dunno. Said his name was Johnny somethin'. Looks like a cowboy—a movin'-pitcher cowboy. Rode up on a horse, an' Sessums give him a job."

Wesley turned a little sick-looking. "That don't worry me none," he said shakily. "Cain't no two-bit stranger get her away from me."

"Well," finished Essie cheerfully, "I got t' be goin'. Jus' thought I'd stop an' talk t' you a minute."

"Pleasant feller, that Essie," Wesley muttered when Driggers walked out of earshot. "Let's wait till he gets out o' sight; I wouldn't have him see me do this for nothin'. But I jus' remembered that I gotta see Matt Sessums about a cotton trailer, too. You wanna go along?"

The road to the Sessums farm wound southwest up Cottonwood Creek. Wesley steered the car across a mesquite-covered draw to a low flat cotton field. "Reckon they're in this field? Yep, I see the trailer an' scales."

The cotton was so high that Cliff could see only a head bobbing up here and there where different members of the Sessums family were sacking it up. Wesley followed bumpy ruts along the turnrow to the trailer, and there stopped the car quickly.

" 'Lo." Annabelle's frying-sized brother named Scud stuck his head around the trailer. He had been guzzling water out of a fruit jar. When he wiped his chin he left a long streak of dirt. "Ya wanna see Annabelle?"

"Mebbe. Where is she?"

Scud grinned. "Down toward th' other end."

Wesley crawled out of the car. He greeted several more of the children glumly as he and Cliff walked by where they were picking. He didn't give Mr. Sessums time to start talking as they hurried by his sack. Soon there were only two pickers in front of them.

Annabelle turned around slowly when Wesley spoke. She had a rather flat face which kept the same expression most of the time, but now there was color in her cheeks. She slipped her bonnet off her pale hair, letting it fluff in the breeze.

" 'Lo, Wesley," she finally answered.

Cliff looked at the man who was picking on the cotton row beside her. Essie Driggers hadn't stretched things, for a wonder. The boy was a stranger, and he was handsome. And his clothes! Such fancy clothes had never been seen in a Red Bluff cotton patch before. Cliff's eyes traveled over the black Stetson, past the navy-blue shirt with leather lacing and red embroidery. There were levis to match, and black boots with multicolored butterflies on the tops. Cliff's eyes met his dark ones. They were set behind lashes as long and curling as a girl's, and there seemed to be laughter hiding somewhere in them.

"Oh," stammered Annabelle, "Cliff an' Wesley, this is Johnny Lemay."

"Johnny what?" Wesley's voice sounded queer. It sounded like a balloon losing air.

"Lemay—it's French."

Johnny smiled. "Glad to meet you. I was lying around my ranch, waiting for roundup, so I thought I'd ride up here and pick cotton for a week or two—jus' to pass the time away." He shook down his sack with an expert hand.

"Your ranch—is it pretty good sized?"

"Rather large," he shrugged.

"Oh—you live far from here?"

"Not too far."

"You oughta hear him play th' git-tar," Annabelle broke in, "an' you oughta hear him sing. I think I'll give a party for him while he's stayin' here with us."

There was a dead silence. Wesley looked from Johnny back to Annabelle. He looked at her hair like a hungry hound would look at a pan of freshly cooked cornbread. "Annabelle," he started out, "I jus' thought I'd come by an' see if you aim to go with me t' singin' Sunday night."

Annabelle looked down. "Well, since I didn't tell you for sure, I think I'll jus' go with th' family this time."

"O.K.," Wesley answered in a low voice. "C'mon, Cliff, let's go."

When they were out of the field, driving back on the main road, Wesley asked, "Cliff, what do you make of it?"

"I don't know." There was a twinkle in Cliff's eyes.

Wesley burst out, "If there's anything I hate, it's a put-on. Why don't that tinhorn cotton picker admit he's a sand lapper like th' rest o' us? Did you see th' way that cottonsack was fillin' up? I'll eat my hat if he wasn't born an' raised in th' cotton patch. But, no, he's got t' be a cowboy—he's got t' be a Frenchman! He's got t' wear fancy clothes an' play th' git-tar! An' I'll bet you before th' week is out ever' gal aroun' Red Bluff will be chasin' after that guy. You'd think women would have more sense."

"Mebbe they will."

"Well," Wesley continued, "I aim t' show that bird up if it's th' last thing I ever do. I aim t' find out where he come from an' go see what kind o' ranch he has."

"Aw, don't be too hard on him," Cliff suggested. "He's probably jus' out havin' fun. He may be a poor boy who hasta get out o' his own community t' put on a show."

"He's gonna wish he'd picked some other place t' put on his show before he's through aroun' here," Wesley answered. "I aim t' show that guy up. I'm not goin' t' be long about it, neither."

Cliff didn't see Wesley for three days; during the time he finished heading the maize. Then one morning he was out in the cow lot milking when Wesley's car stopped in front of the house.

Wesley hurried out to the lot. "Cliff, you done?"

"Sure." Cliff pushed the last calf through a gate and closed it. "What you out so early for, Wes?"

"What you reckon? You ready t' take a trip today?"

"You can't mean about that Lemay guy?"

"Sure. You think I'm goin' t' let him hang aroun' till he gets t' take Annabelle t' singin'?"

"Oh, Wes! In the first place, what use is it? An' in the second place, how would you know where t' go?"

Wesley reached carefully into one pocket. He pulled out a folded piece of paper and handed it to Cliff. Cliff frowned as he read it aloud, " 'Mrs. Luther Lemay, Flat Top, Texas'—what in the world is this, Wes?"

"A return address off a letter," Wesley smiled broadly. "I figgered no matter how much of a skunk a feller is, his mother will always keep track o' him jus' th' same."

"But how in the world did you get hold of it?"

"Don'tcha think Scud is good for somethin'? That kid will do anythin' for a dollar. Lemay's mail comes t' Sessums' box. Th' rest was easy."

"Where's Flat Top?"

"I looked it up. It's acrost over in Parnell County. It won't take us long. C'mon, be a sport."

Cliff picked up the bucket of milk. "All right; let's see if I can slip off without havin' t' cut stove wood."

Finally they were out on the open road headed south. They passed the Red Bluff post office, throwing a little more dust over the faded sign. Down the clay hill they went, across rolling pasture country dotted with drouthy farms.

Across the highway the road began to get rougher. A low range of hills peeped up out of the south. "We're sure in ranch country now," Cliff ventured. "We haven't passed a house in a long time."

The sun climbed higher and chased away the mists from the hills. The road started uphill, winding around chalky slopes. Suddenly Wesley said in excitement, "Lookee back there! I believe that house—had a sign on it!"

They turned around and looked at the bleached sign, FLAT TOP STORE. Wesley stopped the car and hurried inside. In a moment he was back, jerking the cardoor open. "Sure, th' storeman knows Johnny Lemay! Luther Lemay is Johnny's dad. Th' Lemay house isn't far from here. He says Luther Lemay is—" he paused, "herdin' sheep for someone in a pasture over here."

Several miles down the dim, washed-out road Cliff spotted a battered house leaning against some scrub-cedar trees. "Look on the mailbox! Luther Lemay."

"Yep, there it is," Wesley said in satisfaction. "Look 'er over. Ranch, eh?"

"Well, now you've seen it can't we go home?"

"Heck, no! You think I aim t' get cold feet now? I'm goin' up an' get well acquainted with th' folks."

"Wes, you're crazy!"

"I'll learn that guy t' come up t' Red Bluff an' play cowboy."
Wesley drove on in front of the house. A ragged collie dog
crawled out from under the propped-up porch and barked.

A tall, thin woman opened the door, wiping her hands on her
apron. Wesley stepped up the porch, dodging several missing
boards.

"Watch them steps," the woman cautioned him. "The man
who owns this place, he won't fix up nuthin'."

"Are you Mrs. Lemay?"

"Sure. But if you want Luther, he's out at sheep camp." Cliff
could see that Mrs. Lemay had once been pretty.

"Well, we're from Red Bluff, where yer boy is workin'. I'm
Wesley Quitman, an' this here is Cliff Allison. We were jus'
passin' by, so thought we'd stop in."

"Why, boys, I'm glad t' see you! We sure have missed Johnny.
But th' little varmit is real good t' write an' send money home.
Come right in."

Cliff found himself in a clean, plain front room, with dyed
woolsack curtains at the windows.

"That Johnny sure gets restless," Mrs. Lemay was still talking. "He's always got t' be makin' money. We kinda starved out,
raisin' cotton, an' he sure hates t' herd sheep."

"We—" Wesley started to say something, and then he stopped,
for someone else had slipped through a side door into the room.
She was about seventeen. She was wearing old levis and a faded
shirt—and didn't need anything else. She had the same warm,
dark eyes and curving lashes of Johnny, but there the favor
ended. She had a pert, round face, and down her back hung two
long, thick plaits of the prettiest yellow hair Cliff had ever seen.

"This is Charlene," Mrs. Lemay explained.

Charlene smiled. There was a curve of pink lips, and a flickering dimple. "I'm glad to see you. It's awful lonesome here. We most never have any company aroun'. Guess we're too hard to find."

"You—you don't look much like Johnny," Wesley managed to say.

"Wish I could go places an' work like Johnny does. We never have any parties down here. You have any parties where you come from?"

"Yes," Wesley gulped. "Yes, parties an' church an' singin's."

She sighed. "Sure sounds good." She curled up in a chair like a kitten, and the sun reflected on her shining hair.

"Lissen," Mrs. Lemay said, "I was jus' startin' to set out dinner. Charlene made a chocolate cake today, an' we raided the late pea patch. You boys come an' eat with us an' tell us about Johnny."

"Oh, no," Wesley shook his head, but his eyes stayed fastened on Charlene's hair. "We couldn't put you t' no trouble."

"I'll bet you don't like cake, Wes-ley." She moved her chair closer to his.

"Oh, yes, ma'am," Wesley stammered, "I do like cake."

A while past noon Cliff said, "Lissen, Wes, you fixin' t' take up board here? We got a long drive home. Hang up that apron you got wrapped aroun' you and let's start back."

Wesley walked out of the kitchen, sheepishly draping a cup towel over a cane-bottomed chair. "I reckon we got t' go." He kept looking at Charlene, then finally turned and walked out to the car with the blank, vacant stare of a sleepwalker.

"Look out!" cried Cliff as the car began to back away. "Look where you're goin'! You like to have backed over that fence post there."

Wesley slowly steered the car down the lane toward the mailbox.

"Well," Cliff began, "I hope you're satisfied. You found where Johnny Lemay come from, an' now you can go home to Red Bluff an' tell ever'body what a big liar he is."

"Did you see her hair?" Wesley answered. "I never seen hair that color before. Them long braids o' hers make Annabelle Sessums' hair look th' color o' dishwater."

"Now," Cliff continued, "You can make Johnny Lemay sure look sick. You can—"

"An' did you see how she took to me?" Wesley broke in. "I never seen such a sensible gal. An' did you taste that chocolate cake she—"

"Yes, Johnny will be so bumfuzzled he will pack those fancy clothes an' leave right out o' Red Bluff. He—"

"But th' poor, lonesome, little gal—she hasn't been to a party in a long time," Wesley continued, still following his own line of thought.

"An' it isn't hard t' see that she aims t' go t' one," returned Cliff. "I saw her eyin' your car, Wesley—Wes! Can't you see that you're jus' bein' used for a ride somewhere?"

Wesley turned from the wheel with a snarl. "Cliff, you shuddup! I never seen such a suspicious feller. You stuffed yerself on her cake, an' now you accuse her o' workin' me!"

"But what about Johnny?"

"Johnny?" Wesley looked blank again. "Oh, him? Like I said, he's jus' a good, hard-workin' kid, out havin' fun. I was jus' thinkin'—maybe when he finishes pickin' at Sessums', he could pick some fer me. He could borrow my car, t' go visit his folks. I might even drive it fer him, jus' t' help th' boy out—"

"But, Wes—what about Annabelle?"

Wesley frowned. "Annabelle Sessums? That cotton-headed fat thing? Boy, I'm goin' t' quit her while I got a good excuse. I always did say she was too old fer me. You take a young gal, now, you can raise her up t' suit yerself."

Cliff began to laugh.

"What you laughin' at?" Wesley grumbled. "Boy, you jus' wait a year or two—then I'll be laughin' right back at you!" His face turned again to a smile, and his voice trailed off, "An, she don't like 'Blue Yodel No. 2,' neither!"

Interlude at Rancho Alegre

A s Robert Duran rode toward the village of Rancho Alegre, below the Sierra Madres in the state of Chihuahua, Mexico, he was haunted by a feeling of finality—as if he was approaching some way station in his life which might have some degree of meaning or permanence. Or perhaps it was only a hope—spawned in some deep layer of his senses—rather than any emotion born of reason. Such feelings were obviously not shared by the uneven column of Mexican soldiers sprawled on horses behind him, backing up—even in their state of hangover from the last ranch village—the recent agreement between Texas and Mexico to stamp out hoof and mouth disease in cattle. Officially this group was part of the Aftos Commission, but the people of ranches and villages were beginning to call them "Los Matavacas"—"The Cowkillers".

Duran had no illusions as to why he had been promoted from the post of river rider—on the American side—to cattle inspector: he spoke Spanish with a liquid sound, he could sit on a horse for days, he could stomach the blazing food from native villages. Furthermore, he did not affront the native alcaldes with a hearty, overbearing Anglo bluster. He was small, slender, wiry, burned by the sun—with hair as black as any Indian's. Only as Mexicans studied the cast of his features, and noticed the white line on his forehead when he sometimes pushed his hat above the tan, did they realize that he was a foreigner from the north.

He looked back at the soldiers. He had not asked for them—

they were *pelados*—coarse fellows—a nuisance. They had caused a near-riot over some girls at the last cantina, and the natives hated them heartily. Since the ranchers in this district seemed afraid to give trouble about rounding up their cattle and having them inspected and vaccinated—not even when he had had to shoot some of the vast Rancho Boca herd—Duran had decided that he would call back to headquarters from the first telephone he could reach, and try to have most of the soldiers sent back.

The road veered downward, away from high bare slopes into a river course of fertile beauty. A wide stream of water gurgled there, clear and cold, dappled with the shadows of feathery trees. Duran pulled aside under a wild china tree and spoke to the lieutenant in charge of the soldiers. "My map shows that it is not far to the hacienda and village. Let's drink and rest the horses."

The lieutenant reined beside him. "Could we have the siesta here? El Patrón—and the *vaqueros*—will not wish to stir about with cattle in the heat."

"No, the siesta will have to wait. They have been notified to have their cattle penned."

The lieutenant smiled sourly. "No siesta? Señor, you have stayed north of the border too long. Where did you say you were born?"

"Canada. I am French. I came to the United States to train horses, and stayed to work on ranches."

"Then why do you not find a woman among our people, and stay here? The *señoritas* in the villages—are they not pretty?"

"Very."

The lieutenant led his horse to the bank. "You have a woman in the States—maybe?"

"No—not now or ever. I was born in a simple country, I am a simple man. The women of America are not simple."

The lieutenant broke into hearty laughter. "Señor, you say plenty! I have a cousin in Juarez—poor boy. He marry a girl from El Paso, though we warn him many times. *Pobrecito,* he do nothing since but work hard to please her. She must have the cookstove, the washing machine. When she have a baby, she must have the doctor, the nurse, the hospital. The women of Mexico—they ask for nothing. They live to please men. They grind corn, make clothes, carry water, have many babies. Use your brain and find you a woman in Mexico."

Duran changed the subject as he bathed his face, dousing away the brown dust. "This is good cattle country."

"This is below the country of the Tarahumara. These people are stubborn. You may expect trouble."

"Not if we treat them right."

"Nonsense, Señor! These Indian peons have no sense. If it were not for these guns and men, your Border Commission would turn tail across the river."

"I doubt that. We'd better move along."

The hour of siesta lay in a golden calm across the little village down the bend of a valley. Duran felt the peace of it seep inside him. A man could stay here forever, content beside the river. The house of El Patrón stood back against a hill—white plastered adobe, with vast corrals to one side. The village square, with its dusty tamarisk and acacia trees, was flanked by stone and adobe huts of the *vaqueros.*

A servant scurried, mouselike, and peeped out of a heavy cedar door on the big house. "El Patrón Rafael Velarde has finished siesta. You will find him in the courtyard, Señor."

Robert Duran motioned to the lieutenant to hold back his

soldiers. He opened a low gate and walked beside a peach tree which was fragrant with ripening fruit. A man stepped from back of the house to face him. He was silent, with his manner and bearing indicating hostility. He was tall and slender, with the features of Old Spain darkened by a light overprinting of Tarahumara. A large gray dog beside him—an animal which appeared more wolf than dog—snarled at Duran.

"Señor Velarde, I am from the Border Commission. You were delivered our notice. We have come to inspect your cattle. Have you penned them?"

"My cattle are not sick. I will have nothing to do with you people," El Patrón replied. "I have heard how you go about— disturbing our animals and people—breaking our customs. Leave my ranch and never come back."

"Señor—" Duran spoke quietly, "I'm afraid you do not understand. Your animals can appear well in the first stages of the disease, and yet— This is an order of your own government as well as ours, and we are only assisting—"

"Get out of here, you filth!" El Patrón turned to his dog. "Get him!" he ordered in Spanish.

The dog sprang toward Duran, snarling, fangs bared. Duran jumped back in quick amazement. The dog missed his leg, but seized the cuff of his jeans. He bit through them, then yelped and leaped backward when Duran landed a kick on one side.

"Get him!" El Patrón ordered again.

Gasps of surprise came from the soldiers. They began moving in.

"Kill him!" Duran called.

The shot came from the lieutenant, its hot breath whistling past Duran, and ending in a tearing thud. El Patrón crumbled slowly, evenly, with a large hole drilled in the middle of his forehead.

The dog yelped once, then ran behind the peach tree.

Duran leaped forward. "No! What have you done? You've killed him! Can't you see you've killed him?"

"Of course. Isn't that what you asked us to do?"

"No—the dog! The dog! Not the man!"

The lieutenant shrugged. "Señor—what is the difference? He deserved it. These people have no sense." He turned back to the street, where a swarm of natives was quickly gathering. "Get back, you fools! Any hombre who dares to touch one of us will die! Your *patrón* just defied the government of Mexico, the United States, and the soldiers of Chihuahua!"

Duran leaned over El Patrón, clutched his still pulse, and watched the bright blood spread on the cobblestones. "There seems to be nothing we can do for him." He straightened up. "But we can't go on—with this cattle inspection business today. I will have to go somewhere and call headquarters and report this."

"There will be nothing done. I will report that the man resisted and threatened you. Listen, you hombres—" the lieutenant roared to the crowd, "we are leaving now. But we will be back in a few days. And we expect you to have the cattle here in corrals! If you do not—we will take all you have in your houses, pile it in the streets, and burn it. El Presidente will not stand for any more trouble. And the governor of Chihuahua—"

Duran was no longer listening, for a girl was bounding from the house with the quick grace of a deer of the Sierra Madres, materializing at last from his nameless longings. She was amber-skinned and clean-limbed, a creature of both the earth and stars.

He watched her, taken aback by her sorrow and beauty. Her most striking feature was her eyes, sooty, long lashed, stamped faintly with an Oriental cast.

"Papa!" she sobbed. "What have you done to Papa?" She fell beside her father, the curve of her breast heaving. When she straightened, those eyes blazed in her flower-face. Then she brushed back her flowing waves of lustrous dark hair, and studied Duran mockingly. "You filthy gringo," she said. "Get away. Get away and don't ever come back!"

"Do not worry, Señorita," he answered slowly. "I know how to leave."

Transition

Long before summer came to the Red Bluff community that year Cliff Allison's mother had been after him to buy a good suit of clothes. Cliff had seen that there was no use to argue with her, so before she could get hold of the money he had earned from picking cotton he had slipped around and spent it on a saddle.

His dad, Newt, came to his rescue. "Now, Maggie," he said, "the way you take on, a person would think we lived in Concho City, instead of out here in the river breaks. Cliff has lived nineteen years without no fancy pin-striped blue suit, and he's apt to live a while longer. All the rest the boys around here—the Sessums and Driggers and Quitmans—they wear levis and striped shirts. Do you want them to think Cliff is tryin' to act like somebody come?"

Maggie looked thoughtfully at Cliff, from his long straight legs to his wavy black hair. "I always said," she persisted, "that I want folks to notice my boy. Why, with that blue suit from page 240 of Sears Roebuck, Cliff would look like a preacher started somewhere to hold a meeting."

Sunday-night singing was over. But before he dismissed the crowd leader Essie Driggers stepped to the front in the schoolhouse to make an announcement. He climbed up to the low stage, carrying a ragged old hymnbook in one sunburnt hand. The Coleman lamp, sitting uncertainly on a piano, wheezed softly as it sent a yellow glow over the long room full of people. In the front seats sat the older folk—with fingers still gnarled from carrying water in and out of dugouts in West Texas homesteading days. Behind them the children and parents were sandwiched in the school desks, and toward the back the young people sat on benches. Essie saw the long slim length of Cliff Allison draped in a back corner.

"Listen here, folks." Essie brushed away a candlebug fluttering around his lank sandy hair. "Don't fergit our pie supper next Thursday night." He lifted the hymnbook higher. "Can't nobody accuse us Red Bluff folks o' havin' a pie supper just t' have a high-heel time, neither. We got to raise enough money to buy them new Rodeheaver songbooks. Girls, fix your pies in extra-fancy boxes. And, boys,"—he looked toward the bench where Cliff sat—"get out and rustle up some extra girls who can bake pies. Make a raid over toward Hackberry Creek, and Martin's ranch. And be here at sundown, sharp!"

The crowd was dismissed, and began to break up into little groups standing and talking here and there. Cliff sauntered past where the older men stood, out to the dimly lit front porch.

"Who you gonna bring?" someone was asking Wesley Quitman.

"I won't be alone," Wesley bragged. "I got a girl who won't go nowhere without me. None o' you better try to bid me out o' her pie."

Orville Sanders was standing a little apart. Cliff was a bit shy of Orville. Maybe Orville didn't think he was any better than the other boys around Red Bluff, but he certainly gave that impression.

Alvie Ledbetter spoke up with what was in Cliff's mind. "Orville," he said, "you are always blowin' about those town kinfolks o' yours. Why don't you bring one o' your girl cousins to the pie supper?" Alvie smiled, showing his horselike teeth.

Orville flushed. "Oh, Linda wouldn't care about no country pie supper."

"Aw, she might, jus' to help us poor people get some songbooks," Alvie scoffed.

"Well, I'll see about it," Orville agreed stiffly. "I guarantee she would be an eye-opener to some o' you fellers. We haven't got no girls out here like that."

Cliff didn't think much more about Orville and his town cousin. He went home and planted some young cotton that the sand had blown out, and doctored some of his dad's calves for the blackleg.

On Thursday, when he and Newt came in from the pasture at dinnertime, there were some interesting smells drifting from the kitchen. Cliff glanced first at the pine table with the checked oilcloth cover. Then he lifted the cloth off the milk buckets in the cooler. He quickly decided the most likely spot to look was in the oven of the big iron cookstove.

"Git out of that oven, Cliff, boy!" His mother scooted swiftly in front of him. "You menfolk aren't supposed to come peepin' around while I bake my pie for tonight!"

Newt was examining a mixing bowl. "I'll bet it's chocolate."

Maggie's blue eyes twinkled. "Now wouldn't you like to know, Newt Allison!"

"Why—ain't you gonna tell me?" Newt looked peeved. "Here, this ain't fair! Here I hafta buy ever'thing to go in th' blame pie in th' first place. Then I hafta go up to the schoolhouse and buy it back. Or, worse still, accidentally pay a dollar for one o' Opal Sessums' big greasy ol' syrup pies. Essie Driggers is always getting me mixed up in something. Why didn't he jus' ask for donations for them books, instead o' cookin' up this pie supper?"

"That wouldn't be half so much fun." Maggie peeked into the oven, and the tantalizing smell grew stronger. "Run along, Cliff. Listen, I done you up a pair o' levis fresh for tonight. You know," she mused, "I wish you had gone ahead and bought a real wool suit las' fall, like I tole you to!"

"Now, Mom." Cliff walked to the washstand and began to dip up water into the pan. "Please don't start that again. What use have I got with a suit o' clothes?"

"Cliff's right," Newt chimed in. "What you tryin' to make out o' him—a lawyer?"

Maggie shook her head. "I don't care what you say—I still claim ever' boy needs a suit o' clothes! Why, some o' these days somebody aroun' here is liable to die, and what would Cliff wear to the funeral?"

"What difference does it make?" snorted Cliff. "When a feller's dead what does he keer?"

"But, boy," Maggie added softly, "some o' these days you may want to go with some girl."

"Any girl who don't like me in my cotton clothes I wouldn't go with," Cliff answered stoutly.

Essie Driggers had set up a cloakroom in the schoolhouse as a storage place for the pies until time to auction them off. As the crowd began to gather that night he stood at the front door and headed the giggling girls onward. "Hurry up, now," he urged. "Don't let nobody see the box it's in."

Cliff sat on the back seat again, watching the people mill around. He jingled the change in his pocket, wondering whether he had enough to bid on someone's pie and make Wesley have to pay high for it. Not that he wanted to get stuck with a bad pie. He didn't know a girl around Red Bluff whom he really wanted to sit beside and eat pie with.

A strange pause settled on the gathering crowd, starting on the front porch. As it spread around the door Cliff looked up. His gray-blue eyes became sober when he saw why everyone was looking toward the door. A girl was walking in, and behind her came Orville Sanders with a smug smile on his face.

She was a different-looking girl. It wasn't just her dress, though it looked like the petals of a pink rose. It was partly her hair, all brown and shiny and orderly. More than anything it was her white soft skin, which made the other girls in the room look brown and muscular.

Her dark eyes looked right at Cliff. Cliff flushed, for he knew he had been staring. She moved toward the cloakroom, the flustered Essie motioning her there.

Alvie Ledbetter was following her. He looked dazzled. "Orville," he asked quickly, "ain't you gonna introduce anybody?"

"Linda Treeloff," Orville muttered grudgingly, "this is Alvie, and that thing over there is Wesley. The guy on the back seat is Cliff."

Cliff rose quickly, as if someone had pulled an invisible string.

"Now git back, you boys!" waved Essie Driggers. "I don't aim for you to find out what this lady's pie looks like. Gimme your paper sack, miss. I don't like the way Alvie is lookin' at it."

As Linda Treeloff handed over the paper sack holding her pie she turned toward where Cliff stood. "Let's find a place to sit down," she suggested to her cousin in a low voice.

"Here's a seat back here," Cliff was surprised to hear himself saying.

"Thank you."

There was a musical quality in her laugh, but she looked at Cliff curiously. With a flutter of the rose-petal dress, she sat down on the rough bench. Cliff caught a glimpse of real silk stockings and tiny high-heeled pumps.

Essie Driggers was trying to get the crowd's attention. "Now lissen, folks," his high-pitched voice began. "We are shore glad to see such a good crowd out. First, now, we will be favored with a special song—"

Linda's disturbing profile leaned nearer. "Were you saving this seat for someone special?"

"Oh, no," Cliff blurted. "You are the most special thing who ever sat here!"

Sitting beside her, he couldn't help noticing the difference in their clothing. A dress such as she was wearing went with— some kind of light wool suit like those that town guys wore in the summertime. He looked with sudden shame at his levis. They were faded, and a little stained where his mother's iron had been too hot.

Essie held the first pie up, where all could see. It was wrapped in white crepe paper, with big lavender ribbons tied on top. "Lookee here," Essie exclaimed, "I'll bet this is a mouth-waterin' cocoanut, all piled with—"

"Fifty cents," bid Newt.

"Seventy-five," someone raised him.

"One dollar," Newt went higher.

There was a long moment of silence. Then—"Sold," Essie finished. "Lemme see, what's the name on that tag? Sold, to Newt Allison, Opal Sessums' pie."

Cliff watched Linda's face as the pies were brought out one by one. Alvie was closely watching her too. But several more were sold before Essie, with a great show of mystery, pulled a

froth of pink paper and ribbons from its brown paper sack.
"Now lookee here," he said in awe. "If the insides of this is half
as good as the outsides, it ought to be fit for a congressman.
Now who will—"

"Two dollars," broke in Alvie Ledbetter.

"Three dollars," Cliff said anxiously.

Alvie leaned over toward him. "I'm gonna put you out o'
this," he muttered.

Linda frowned at Alvie, her straight little nose tilting slightly.
Everyone turned around as Alvie said loudly—"Five dollars!"

Cliff felt nervously of his change. He could not raise the bid.
He did not have five dollars. But as he stared silently at the
upraised box with its dainty paper and ribbons something began
to look a little familiar about it. Hadn't he seen some ribbons
like that in Mom's sewing-machine drawer at home? He felt a
light touch on his arm, and heard Linda whisper—"That isn't
my pie!"

"Sold!" Essie announced. "Sold to Alvie Ledbetter—for five
dollars—Mrs. Newt Allison's pie."

Alvie's face changed color. It went pale, then a light purple.
But he stood up, and stumbled weakly forward to take the box.

"At least," Cliff whispered smilingly to Linda, "Ol' Alvie is
gettin' a good pie."

"My pie," she volunteered, "is in a little plain white box."

"That one there?"

"Yes."

When all the pies were sold, the eating began. Cliff placed
Linda's pie on a school desk and carefully lifted the box top.

"Oh, dear!" she moaned. "Look, it's all shaken up!"

"Oh, it's pretty," Cliff assured her. He took his pocketknife
and began to saw at a slice. The knife gripped at the crust, but

failed to make headway. Cliff bore down harder, and gouged out a piece. Out of the corner of one eye he could see Alvie Ledbetter watching him sourly, and his dad keeping a wary eye on him.

"Boy, this is sure good," he said loyally as he took a bite. "I always did like—orange pie. Say, I'm sure glad you came tonight."

"Lime pie," she corrected sweetly. "And I'm glad I came, too."

There must have been something wrong with his taste, for he might as well have been eating moonshine. "You—you live in town, don't you?" he stammered. "Can I see you again some time?"

She was looking at his cotton clothes. "Oh, sure," she said evasively, "maybe we'll run into one another—around Main Street sometime."

"But I'd like," he explained humbly, "to go to your own house and see you."

She did not answer.

It was late. Cliff and Newt and Maggie were jogging along toward home in the Model T. "I was talkin' to you, son," Maggie repeated. "I said, what did you think of the pie supper?"

"Think?" A vision floated before his eyes; it danced in a rose-petal dress in front of the car headlights.

"I noticed how you took to that fancy-dressed town girl," Newt broke in. "Now, Cliff, you're just askin' for trouble, throwin' yourself at a girl like that. I'll bet she don't give a flip for—"

Cliff heard no more. He steered the car under the chinaberry trees in front of the house. Soon he was swinging up the front porch with long strides. While his mother lit the coal-oil lamp he fumbled around in a corner under a big pile of magazines.

"What you doing with the Sears and Roebuck?" asked Newt. "Come on, let's get to bed. My stomach feels like it's floatin' over and over. I'll bet I dream about a syrup mill all night."

"I was jus' looking here in the catalogue," Cliff answered softly and without looking up. "You know, Mom, like you said, every boy ought to have a suit of clothes."

"Suit of clothes! Agrivation!" snorted Newt. "Boy, you must o' got poisoned on that green-colored pie you ate! Talkin' about suits—in this hour of the night—and in June! You know we got no money in June! We got to cut corners until cotton picking time!"

Maggie walked across the room. She took the catalogue from Cliff, and held it in her strong brown hands. She looked quietly at her son, a warm light springing in her faded eyes. "Newt," she began carefully, "to listen at you talk, you were born a grown man. Don't you sit there and play like we're broke! And me with a whole flock of settin' hens to be culled out and sold any night Cliff can catch them. Where were you lookin', boy? On page 240?"

Matters of Preference

Matt Sanco had never noticed Clara Tracy much until one October afternoon at the Red Bluff general store. He had seen her around at parties and at Sunday-night singings, without ever having realized how pretty she was. But this afternoon he was driving back from the cotton gin in town, with an empty trailer clattering behind his dad's pickup. Just in front of the post office, where a faded sign said RED BLUFF, TEXAS, one of the trailer tires went flat. Matt's brown young face reflected disgust when he crawled out of the pickup to look it over. He started the pickup, and rattled it to the air hose in front of the store.

"Hello, Mr. Loper," he nodded to a neighbor who was leaning against a gas pump. He walked across the flat concrete porch, and pushed back a screen door.

Clara stood beside the counter. She was a small, slim thing, with hair just as dark as Matt's. It was waved and feathery, and fell away from her oval face and big gray eyes. As Matt looked into those faintly slanting eyes, he saw that they were the color of smoke curling up from a mesquite campfire. But he must have gazed into them too long, for he felt suddenly as if he had plunged into river water just over his head.

When he came up for air it was her dress that caught his eye. He figured she must have held out some money on her dad from picking cotton in order to buy it. It was an apricot-colored dress —just about the color of the frost-bitten cottonwood leaves on the creek in front of Matt's home.

"Hello, Clara." He spoke softly.

"Hello, Matt." She gave him a long, sideways glance.

"Could I buy you a soda pop?"

"They don't have the kind I want." She lifted the ice-chest top. "But I reckon I'd better take second choice. Second choice is better'n none. I'll take an orange."

Matt opened it for her, and nodded to her dad, Ronnie Tracy, who was picking up a box of groceries. Matt glimpsed economical things—rice, beans, and corn meal.

"I'll help you carry that stuff to the car, Mr. Tracy," he ventured.

Clara followed them across the porch. "Matt," she asked suddenly, "will I see you at church?"

"Sure," he answered, "I'll be there."

Later, as Matt drove down the road from Red Bluff to his own home, he kept thinking of Clara Tracy. He had heard people say: "Clara would be the prettiest girl in the country—" but they always added, "—if she had any decent clothes to wear!" The longer Mr. Tracy rented farms around the countryside the poorer choices he seemed to have. Just this year the Tracy family had moved into a worn-out, blown-out shinnery place north of Rattlesnake Canyon. Ronnie Tracy wasn't overly fond of work—his mind running more to hound hunts—but he was certainly fond of seeing that all seven of his family kept busy. Almost any time you drove down the road near his place you would see Clara and the younger children in the field.

Matt herded the pickup over rattling Cottonwood Creek bridge. On the other side, flanked by low hills, stood his own white-painted frame home. The massive pecan trees in front almost hid Bert Loper's car.

" 'Lo, Matt," Loper greeted him a few moments later. "I beat you from the store. Your dad around?"

"Al's driving in the cows, Bert," Matt's mother called from the front porch. "Matt, did you leave my crate of eggs at the Red Bluff store?"

"Oh, Mom!" Matt exclaimed, "I clean forgot to take those eggs out of the pickup. I don't know why I plumb forgot 'em like that!"

"It wouldn't be hard to guess the reason," smiled Bert. "I'll bet the reason wore a yeller dress."

Matt grinned. They sat down on the porch steps. "Matt," Bert burst out again, "you don't have the sense God promised a grasshopper! You never will have no girl, at the rate you're going!"

"I won't?"

"Heck, no, boy! When I was your age, no little black-headed gal could of switched around me in Red Bluff store and got out without having a date made! Why I heard Clara Tracy ask you if you was going to church, and you just up and walked off like a big horse."

Matt shook his head. "What makes you think I want to go with that girl?"

"Boy, are you crazy? That's the very kind of girl you ought to go with! Always pick on a poor girl, like Clara Tracy! A poor girl ain't stuck-up and hard to please. A poor girl appreciates what you do for her."

"Might be something to that."

'They is. Don't ever pick on a girl who has too easy a time at home. Pick on some hard-working little girl who ain't used to nothing. It will save you lots of misery and money."

"Reckon she'd go with me?"

"Boy—that little gal would jump at the chance to get out of the cotton patch."

Five days passed before Matt had an excuse to drive over to where the Tracys lived. The morning was cool, with gusts of wind breathing from the north. The road to their place leading around the curve of the river to where they lived was almost rough enough to loosen Matt's teeth. It wound between shinnery thickets, and red-clay draws, and big gray sandrock. As Matt neared the house, he pulled beside a sandy field. The cotton was skimpy and frost-bitten.

"They must be eating dinner," Matt observed when he passed a pile of empty cottonsacks beside the scales. He drove around a clump of catclaw bushes in front of the mailbox.

Clara stood beside the mailbox, clutching a half-opened package in her hands. She was wearing an old blue dress, and a slat bonnet had fallen back from her matted black hair. When she saw Matt, warm color flooded into her cheeks.

"Hello," she said when he stopped the car. "I was just getting the mail."

"Get in, and I'll drive you to the house."

"I'm too dirty." Yet she crawled into the door he pushed open. "We've been in the field all morning."

"You about done picking?"

"Ought to be. We're having to chase it down."

He steered the car up sandy ruts between scrub oak. Clara tore eagerly into her package. "Dad gives me a little of my money that I get from picking cotton," she explained. "I ordered me another dress."

"If it looks as good as that yellow dress you was wearing at the store," Matt ventured, "it will be mighty pretty."

Clara became downcast. "That yellow dress? It may be pretty, but I didn't want that color. I ordered a red one, and they sent second choice." She rustled the package, then she sighed. "Would you believe it? It always happens to me! Look at this!" She slowly pulled out a green dress. "Listen to this letter! 'We regret that we have to substitute'—Big, fancy words. But they just mean—second choice again!"

"Send it back," suggested Matt.

"Isn't that just like a man!" She smiled wanly. "I've tried that before! And what always happens—I have to wait a long time, and finally get a letter saying the shipment didn't ever come through! So I end up with something a lot worse—or nothing. Send it back? Not on your life! I'll wear green and like it!"

Matt stopped the car in front of a low house with a sagging porch across the front. Several long blue hounds half rose and began to bay.

"Shuddup," Ronnie Tracy muttered to the hounds. He ambled across the creaking porch boards. When he tossed down a piece of dry cornbread the hounds dived toward it. "Daughter, where you been? We're near done eating. You can't scrap cotton without dinner." He silently opened the front door for Matt.

"That's what I wanted to see you about," explained Matt. "We need somebody to help us pick cotton three or four days."

He sat down in the cane-bottomed chair Mr. Tracy glumly offered. As he looked around, he saw that someone who liked pretty things had worked hard on that room. On the bare scrubbed floor lay a big rug plaited out of bright rags. At the windows hung some curtains made from burlap sacks, and a sweet-potato vine climbed out of a glass jar. He tried to keep from staring at an old car seat which had been padded and covered with bright cotton print.

"You done with your cotton?" Matt asked again.

"Not yit," said Mr. Tracy. "And then I promised Sessums we'd help him."

"Well, that's too bad." Matt stood up. "I'll not keep you any longer."

"You been to dinner?"

"Yes, thank you, Mr. Tracy."

Clara walked to the door beside him. Her voice was soft and inviting. "Goodbye."

"Listen, Clara." He was almost whispering. "I been wanting to ask you to go somewhere with me. Could you go riding with me sometime?"

A light slowly flickered behind her gray eyes. She studied Matt appraisingly, with that strange, sidewise gaze. "Why sure," she answered. "Not at night, for I have to milk cows. But sometime in the day. Could we drive to town?"

Matt was able to take her driving sooner than he had expected. One morning a slow drizzle crept out of the southeast; it dampened the cotton too much for picking, but didn't muddy the roads. Matt dressed up, poured some rose hair oil on his hair, and hurried over to the Tracy home.

Sitting in the car beside Clara, headed down the winding road toward the county seat, Matt caught the scent of talcum powder filtering through her new dress. It made him fell light-headed, just as he had felt the time he had slipped into Bob Sessums' homemade wine.

She snuggled against him, squeezed his arm. "Here's the edge of town. Do we have to hurry?"

"Why no, if you don't want to."

"Then turn off the highway and drive sort of slow through

town; through the part where people live. I like to look at town houses."

Matt felt acutely puzzled, but he obediently veered his car off the highway and toward a residential street. "Up this way?"

"No, not here. Keep driving till the houses look really nice." Her face turned away from Matt, toward the window. "Look at that house there! Oh my, what pretty windows! And that porch! I'll bet they have a cute kitchen, too! You know when I was little, I used to believe that someday I would really live in a pretty house in town. I hoped I'd never have to work in the field. I hoped I'd have pretty clothes and a yard full of flowers."

"And why can't you?" asked Matt.

"Me—raised in the cotton patch—ever have a nice town house?" she smouldered. "I wouldn't even know how to meet a town man, or what to say to one! I don't have a chance! Oh, you don't know—you've had it easy. You—the only child in the family, with a nice place to live and all that. I know where I stand, I'll do well to ever have a nice country house!"

"Mebbe," Matt broke in, "you could catch some town guy. You are a pretty girl."

She was looking at a brick house. It was set behind a big lawn and clipped hedges. "What decent town guy," she asked, "would look at a girl in an ordered dress? And—look at my hair! And look at my legs!"

"Sure would like to," Matt grinned, "but I have to drive."

She stretched out one leg. Underneath the service-weight hose long red scratches showed, scratches made from cottonstalks and burrs. "What's the use of my talking?" she burst out. "What made me say all those fool things? Forget it, forget it. Let's go to a show."

Inside the theater, Clara sat quietly. There was something remote about her profile as she toyed with the popcorn Matt handed her. She spoke little until they were driving out of town several hours later, back northwest again, over a batten rim of hills, skimming along the river. Then she smiled, and snuggled against Matt.

Finally they reached Cottonwood Creek. Clara's eyes roved over the creek bottoms and hills. They fastened upon Matt's home. "Your folks have a very nice house, Matt. It's painted, and it's got nice shade trees. And the land around is not bad; it will always raise cotton."

Matt turned and looked at her. He saw the cloud of hair, the slant of her eyes. "Sure," he said, "we like it."

For one night, two weeks later, Matt's dad had planned a coyote hunt. About sunset Matt began to call up the dogs. He blew a long note on the curved cow horn, and White Man and Wolf Bait answered from the creek. "Dad, did you say Loper was going too?"

"Sure, you couldn't tie the old varmint away. He always has to be the big cheese at any to-do. Got out the coffee, Myrtle?"

"I have," Matt's mother answered. "The way you menfolk fret over this hunt is a sight." She sat down to rest on the rock cistern rim. "Don't I hear Loper's car coming?"

Bert Loper turned his car in through the front gate, and let it come to rest underneath the burnished pecan trees. "Look how them leaves are falling off," he remarked as he crawled out. "I tell you, it's gonna be a hard winter. Shuddup, Hula Girl," he growled at the pack of dogs crammed in the back seat. "No, sir, you can't get out now! And if you chase skunks tonight, I'll whup you ever' one!" He turned toward the porch. " 'Lo, Myrtle, 'lo, Al, 'lo, Matt. Did I beat ever'body here?"

"Sure did, Bert. Matt, get Bert a chair."

"Don't bother," Bert swung his lean frame down on the steps beside Matt. "I'm so dawg tired I could rest anywheres. I don't know why I'm going on this fool hunt. Who else is going?"

"Oh, Sessums, Poteets, Wilson—"

Bert chuckled, "No Tracys in th' bunch?"

Matt's face reddened slightly.

"I reckon it wouldn't pay," Bert continued. "From what I hear, the poor little gal is grieving her heart out over Matt. She told someone that Matt went with her once and then never did come back. She couldn't figger why; she was all broke-up over it. Matt boy, what in the world do you mean? A pretty little girl—a pretty little poor girl who has had a hard time and would appreciate anything you did for her—"

Matt cleared his throat.

"I give up," Bert finished. "I'm plumb disgusted with you. If you ever aim to marry, you missed your chance."

"Hush up!" Myrtle interrupted. "Let the boy grow up!"

Al laughed. "If Myrtle has her way the boy never will grow up! But why are we sitting here? We've got coffee, and a wash-tub full of ice in the kitchen, with bottles of soda pop floating in it. Bring us some, Myrtle."

Matt's mother walked to the kitchen, and came back with several bottles of orange soda pop. "Here, Bert, I opened this one for you. And Matt—" She handed one to him.

"Mom, do you have any kind besides this?"

"Why, Matt, boy, I thought orange was your favorite."

"Aw, it used to be," he answered. "But someway, tonight, I believe I'll go hunt me out a grape or something."

The Mesquite

Today I walked among the mesquite thickets. The scent of their softly burning candles of bloom had filtered into every crevice of the countryside. It was strange how such a simple reminder of a half-forgotten spring in Texas could roll back the tides of the inaccessible past. Lost, cherished faces again appeared; old friends walked raw hills in the freshness of their youth. There were stories from every life, and this was one from my own—

Or *was* this myself—Adele Conrad—this smooth-cheeked, tangle-haired, impulsive child of eighteen who sat during morning church services in battered old County Line schoolhouse? I know every inch of the building, for here I had learned to read and write. It was also a fine location for a church; one could peer out the wide windows from the hilltop and see a perfect backdrop for the story of Moses leading the Children of Israel through the desert toward the Promised Land. Upon this particular spring morning, however, the hills were softened with sweet and secret wild lupines and lilies and sand verbenas.

The Union Sunday School, which some of my family belonged to, met on Sunday afternoons. The Christian Church of the community considered the worship of this motley group hardly proper, so they held special services in the morning. Afterward, with clear consciences, members could come back and visit with the other bunch.

I twisted in the narrow school seat and glanced down toward my dress. It was a sheer blue-and-white dimity; the deft fingers of my mother always arranged for her daughters to dress more presentably than other young ladies of this rural area. The pleats of this dress flared gracefully with every motion. It should impress—someone.

My interest in attending morning church services had begun quite recently, and just might have had something to do with the fact that the church leaders belonged to a neighboring clan named Harper. Of course Troy—the youngest son—had never bothered to grace the gatherings with his presence. But this morning he was nearby; I could glance out the window and see him slowly pacing across the hill in the warm sunlight while the services droned on.

I studied the low, worn stage at the front of the room. Troy's father, John Harper, stood behind a homemade pulpit. Someday, if the youngest son behaved himself, he might appear just as distinguished. Mr. Harper had once owned a fine farm in the blacklands of East Texas; present frugal circumstances had not dented his gracious manner.

His voice, gentle, yet with the persuasion of a leader of the British House of Lords, became more earnest. He shook his flowing mane of black-and-silver hair. Never mind that frayed spot in his fine white shirt; Mrs. Harper had mended that so carefully that it could scarcely be seen.

I glanced where she patiently looked toward the front. She was a little armful of a woman with blue eyes which glowed with some sort of inner wisdom. White hair gleamed above her frilly lavender dress, and her warm smile whispered of an understanding heart.

I observed the Harper sons scattered about the audience. They appeared to be decent characters, with wives and children who looked decidedly unbrowbeaten. There was some sort of motto here: once a Harper was captured he stayed captured, and might even become tame!

I was suspicious that six other young ladies sitting about this room were not visiting the church with the slightest intention of hearing John Harper talk. And it was an ironic fact that they were probably appearing more pious than *I* was, even though they were casting the same sidelong glances out the window. Even sultry Maxine Roper—from Shepherd's Crossing—appeared as innocent as a half-opened cactus flower. Among the girls was blonde Opal—gray-eyed and even plainer than I was. If I had been evil-minded I would have said that Troy Harper's business was a bit complicated at this point!

Troy Harper was the only local boy who had ever interested me, and I should leave him alone—no doubt about it. In the first place, he had scattered all my carefully laid plans to leave the community and further my ambitions in the big world which lay beyond the Upper Colorado watershed. And the last thing I really wanted to do was become seriously entangled with a local boy, and lose my chance to escape from the world I had known.

I had tried to analyze his charm. I had seen more imposing men. He was a restless, slender, intense lad of twenty-one, with a face which was a mixture of Robin Hood and an Irish poet. He had a mat of wavy dark hair that tumbled over gray-blue eyes— eyes that always seemed to be searching some distant horizon. When with him, I caught tantalizing glimpses of a complex character: a queer tangle of inner sensitivity—oddly at variance with his station in life—and an overload of earthy honesty and stability which put weights on my wings. He was gay, and witty, and keen-minded, illumed by occasional flashes of hot temper—and I shouldn't bother with him at all.

John Harper lowered his magnificent head for the closing

prayer. When the last echoes ebbed away, the six girls made a calculated dash for Mrs. Harper. I dashed for no one. I slowly strolled across the front porch and down the steps.

I wished someone would explain to me why I had to be so aware of Troy. The other people and the hill became as remote as a dream.

"Hello." He studied me soberly, with just the flicker of a smile gathering in his eyes. "Did you decide to come down from your castle today, and seen how the common, ordinary folk of County Line live?"

"I find the Harper family, with one notable exception, very nice. Why didn't you come inside the church? The lesson was on the Prodigal Son. You would have found it most interesting."

His chin tightened. "Don't you talk to me about religion. You see how far religion has brought my dad. He used to feed everyone in the county where we lived—now watch him hump behind a cottonsack on a rented farm! Don't talk to me about religion."

"I think you are dodging the point. Is religon supposed to make everyone rich?" I shooed away a soft, warm breeze caressing my cheeks. "I have decided that the truth of the matter is that you don't like *any* organized group which might possibly tell *you* what to do!"

"You're so right. I don't!" The light deepened in his eyes. "But I didn't stop your blue-eyed self here to argue with you. What have you done to your hair—it's more shiny-brown and curly than usual. But say, there is a more important thing I want to know—why wouldn't you let me kiss you Thursday night?"

I felt my face grow warmer than the breeze. I managed to meet the straight gaze from his eyes. "I did not like the way you treated me. I am not accustomed to having someone drive me to a far curve of the river, pull the car to one side, turn off the key, and then reach out both arms for me. Listen here, you! You have danced out the nights across the county—you have thrown away every shred of last fall's money you could rake and scrape. You have given pretty Shepherd's Crossing and Sharon Ridge and Lone Wolf girls a spin. Now don't think you can come back and take the ideas you have picked up and use them on me!"

I didn't know that blue eyes could be as stormy as a hailcloud. He reached out and clamped one brown hand on my arm. "You didn't answer my question. Why wouldn't you let me kiss you?"

"No man kisses me unless I love that man," I answered.

"Now we're getting down to facts." He smiled faintly. "And the local yokels don't give that heart of yours a spin—is that it, child. May I carry you back to your castle?"

"No, I'm walking home. Don't ask me to ride with you. Something tells me you will be very, very busy. Isn't this a case of one's chickens coming home to roost?"

We both looked toward the Harper car. Troy's expression became most quizzical.

The situation was obvious. No juggling inside the United States Congress could have matched that of six determined young ladies. They were surrounding the car containing Mr. and Mrs. Harper, and it was plain they all intended to get inside.

Maxine Roper broke away and sauntered toward us. She flicked back a long, dusky wave from the pert roundness of her face. "Troy—aren't you going home today? All of us are going home with your mother and stay until late. And we are getting tired of standing on this hot hill!"

"Now that's a terrible trial for a poor little thing like you," Troy agreed. "But don't you think I'm worth it?"

" 'Course you are." She lifted her dainty, *un*freckled nose. "Is *she* going too?"

"Ease your troubled mind," I answered. "*I* am going home."

Troy reached out one hand toward me. "Get in the car where you belong, Adele."

I pulled away. "Go on with your harem."

When he spun me around his arm felt like a steel band. I looked toward Mrs. Harper, and her little nose was wrinkled with laughter. While I hesitated, Troy grabbed and shoved me underneath the wheel on the driver's side. As he scooted in beside me, I was mashed between himself and the explosive Maxine. I could fell her smoky, tilted eyes studying me at close range, and judged she was drawing satisfaction from the scrutiny. I assumed she had a dagger in her homemade purse.

Troy steered the overburdened car down the road. "It will take a can opener to get us out of this thing," he muttered. He nudged me with one inflexible elbow. "You are going to singing with me back at the schoolhouse tonight, you know."

The atmosphere inside the car became more tense.

"Now don't waste your time trying to argue with a Harper," he continued. "I'll leave you at your house now. But I will be back at sundown—or earlier."

"I won't be around."

I didn't really mean to lie to him. There were many places I meant to go and escape. But I suddenly discovered, as the day wore on, that I wasn't really well enough to go with my family to Union Sunday School—or to town afterward. Yet I was quite well enough to pace across the south side of the creek near my home, and try to sort out the turmoil boiling in my mind. I was fighting the uncanny feeling that part of myself had gone away with that engaging, aggravating driver of the old car full of girls. I couldn't figure out why he should be so attractive, or myself so secretly responsive, and there wasn't anyone I could discuss it with. So I finally limped home, and sat upon the porch to cool my hard-pressed feet. I realized suddenly what a complicated world I had been thrust into without my pre-consent.

I heard the rattle of that familiar car. I allowed myself to give a grudging glance. Troy Harper reached the front gate and made the bow of a stranger seeking entry across a drawbridge.

I should feel stiff and self-conscious around the rascal—I always had around every other boy. But I didn't. I could relax and be myself completely and go on shaking sand from my shoes without apology. I noticed that Troy looked a bit pale and drawn.

He shrugged, and sat down on the floor of the porch. "Fine day, isn't it? I have been walking the river; you have been walking the creek. Can't we get together on this thing, and walk the same direction at least?"

"Walking?" I asked with bewilderment. "Do you mean to say that you haven't been sitting around strumming the guitar and smiling at the girls all afternoon?"

"Girls?" He ran swift fingers through his waves of hair. A lock escaped, as usual, and fell across his forehead.

"Yes, girls. My friend, I have been warned about you. You go dashing around with young things until all hours of the night, and then turn them loose on dark roads to walk home."

He grinned. "Do you believe everything Opal says?"

"What else can I believe? But I have been warned more about that stubborn chin of yours than anything else. 'Stubborn as the Devil,' they call it."

He rocked with laughter. "What do you want—some bowing, scraping, simpering thing to hang onto your dress tail?"

I giggled. "That would be a novelty, at least. And I have also been warned that you said no woman would ever own you."

"I did say that, and I meant it. No woman will ever own me, and I don't want any woman who is so silly that I will completely own her."

"Lovely business arrangement you have figured out. You'll keep a wife around, just as long as you can continue to do as you please. You *are* a strange one. But the man who pleases me must share everything with me—and I mean the beautiful things of life that most people don't even notice. And most importantly—I must mean everything to him."

Troy laughed heartily. "Don't sit there and try to feed me silly ideas like that. But Opal does talk too much. If you were picking out the most dangerous of all those six girls, which would you pick?"

"Maxine, of course. She's about as sweet as a two-year-old wildcat from Cedar Canyon."

Merriment flooded his whole face. "You are just jealous of her, child. But you're wrong. The most dangerous kind of woman is a plain, nosy one who talks too much." He eased nearer by my perch, and picked up one of my shoes. "But I came by to let you know that you and I are starting out on a little ride. It's going to last until night and singing time. Algerita berries from the river are going to make a light supper—how about sneaking out a little bit of your mother's good cooking before we start?"

"I might find a pie. But I don't want to go anywhere with you alone anymore."

"But I have provided two proper chaperones for you—Crockett Black and Irene Trevey."

"That helps," I agreed grudgingly. "Anything would beat sitting around home, I suppose."

Troy remained unusually docile and silent until the car clattered up the hill north of my home. Then he gulped the last bite of pie and resumed. "I forgot to explain—Crockett and Irene aren't going to join us until tonight at singing. Are you going to stay with me?"

I frowned. "What else can I do—jump out of the car? When I'm kidnapped—I'm kidnapped."

An electric silence settled across us both. I glanced at Troy quizzically as the fragrant miles slipped by. We passed the County Line schoolhouse, and crossed a bridge curving above a chasm of the river. Finally he opened a gate to a dim pasture road which led toward a forbidding territory known as "The Cat Den." Not only wildcats resided there, I had heard, but bootleggers and misfits.

"Are you sure someone won't take a shot at us over here?"

"No. They know me here."

"When do we reach our destination?" I didn't trust that distilled mixture of sage and mesquite bloom carried on the breeze. Even the torn old cedars had hopefully thrust out fresh branches.

"When I get to where I can talk to you without someone interrupting."

"We are both wasting our time. We hardly speak the same language. But if you intend to make love to me, I could give you several hints. You could begin by gently telling me how beautiful I am."

"But you are *not* beautiful," he replied. "I don't know *what* you are! I wish you were beautiful and silly—then I could forget all about you."

I laughed heartily, and studied Troy while he swerved the car around a chaparral limb full of thorns. "I'll be more generous with you. I'll admit that you look fairly presentable and romantic.

You even have long, dark eyelashes—in case you haven't known it all your life! You have a profile which is sort of tender and strong at the same time. It's no wonder girls flutter about you— they are stupid enough. But is this the famous Harper line I've been hearing about? Why are you so matter-of-fact with me?"

"Because you are not like other girls I have known. You have more sense, so I come to you with honest talk." He drew a deep breath. "I have a deal to offer you." He stopped the car beside a mesquite tree. Oblique darts of sunlight stabbed through its lacy leaves. "First, let me explain about the Harpers. You see how stubborn we are. We never change. When one of us gets his head set on a woman, it stays there a lifetime."

"Tell me—" I interrupted, "do men ever love their wives?"

His smile turned wry. "Why do you have to jump ahead of me that way? It depends on what you call love. If you mean a lot of fancy, flowery stuff—that passes away." He reached out the car, broke off a twig with creamy bloom, and handed it to me. "This is a pretty thing, you see. But it won't last one day. If it were not for the limb and root these blooms are fastened to, they wouldn't mean much, I want something for us which will never die." I was forced to look into the stormy eyes beneath the black lashes. "But if you mean honor—and being dependable—and never looking at another woman—and being able to go through any hardship together—that is real love."

I stared at those brooding eyes. "Hardship? Dependable? How dull can you get? I have never planned to be the wife of a poor rancher. You can take that kind of a future and sink it in the river! I'll take music and poetry—and so long as I live there's going to be flowers and romance coming from somewhere —or I'll go out and find some so help me! I do not elect to wash your dirty socks and milk cows while you plow!"

Now he was really angry. Blue fire lit those eyes. "You don't know the first lesson in romance! If you'd use that tousled head for more reasoning and less dreaming you'd be a sight better off! And to think that I supposed we could understand each other without even talking!" He started the car, and gave an icy turn to the wheel. "Go to school and make a play for some banker's son. Live in a square house, belong to the country club, and order your flowers from a greenhouse. The next girl I pick will be a human being."

We did not speak while he steered the car back the rough trail which led to the main community road. Long shadows lapped ahead of us across the dust.

We had disturbed another car on the road. It was an unfamiliar vehicle to me, and neither did I recognize the man under the wheel. He was muscular and brown, and he was obviously furious. To my surprise, Opal sat beside him. When she looked at me I heard her shrill giggle.

"The girls must have disbanded for the day," I murmured.

"She's with Roan Shook," Troy spat. He slowed the car.

"Repulsive thing," I murmured.

"Worse than me?"

"Maybe. Where's he from—Shepherd's Crossing?"

"Sure thing. I guess he's hunting for me."

Something about the quiet, cool way Troy said this made me aware of an undercurrent I did not understand.

"I've had trouble with him before. He thinks he's in love with Maxine Roper, and that I took her away from him."

"Why does he keep looking at you that way? Does he want to fight?"

"I don't know. I'm not going to pick trouble with him, but if he comes to this car he'll get enough to interest him."

A game began which was at first laughable, and finally disturbing. The hulking man would steer his car around us, then fall behind. Then he would speed up again and run in front. During one such excursion I heard Opal shriek, "That Troy Harper ought to have his head knocked off for the mean things he's done!"

"What mean thing did you do to her?" I inquired.

He ignored my question, and kept his eyes on our follower. Soon the offending car skidded to a stop in our pathway. We could do nothing but halt behind him. "I think he's a big coward." Troy whispered. "He won't fight fair."

The solid block of a man slowly approached our car.

"What do you want?" Troy asked.

"You're too yellow to step out and learn," replied a guttural drawl.

When Troy left the car he went out hitting. He hit Roan Shook so hard that it rocked him far back on his heels.

Not for long! The big fellow bounced upward, and I saw what had been hidden behind his back all the time. He swung a car crank—a heavy bolt of iron weighing around ten pounds—in a wide arc and crashed it with all his might against Troy's forehead!

I had not realized the viciousness of the fight until this moment. My mother had done her best to shelter me from the more elemental experiences of the County Line community. So this fight had happened so unexpectedly that it jarred my thinking.

The crank caught Troy in the head right across the hairline, and he was badly hurt. Blood spurted down across his eyes, and dripped off his chin. He rocked backward and almost crumbled to the ground. But then he came up, and was still fighting; grabbing for the iron, slugging, taking another glancing blow.

I jumped from the car to hunt rocks, sticks, anything. "The gun!" Troy gasped. "Get the gun from the car pocket!" I grabbed the pistol by the handle. But Roan was running now, and I could see why. Troy had a long knife in his hands, and the blade was open.

Roan raced to the car and spun away. He left Troy staggering behind it in the thick dust. Troy crumbled forward and put his head in his hands.

I knelt beside him, and mopped at his head with the skirt of my dimity dress. "That horrible—crazy thing! Get in the car—come on! I'll have to take you somewhere! Take my handkerchief. I'll have to tear off part of my dress. Let's go see your mother and dad!"

"Don't you tear that pretty dress. I'll be all right." He walked to the car, shoved me under the steering wheel, and fell forward with his bloody head in my lap. "Drive me home."

The Harper home stood on a long hill beyond a field where maize and cotton rotated. As I stopped the car in front of the house, Troy revived and staggered through the flaming sunset toward the door. I followed him inside while the Harper clan stepped aside in astonished silence. The house was orderly and clean. Substantial old furniture inherited from better days graced the bare, scrubbed floors.

We made our silent, uncertain trek to a bedroom, where Troy dropped upon a hand-tufted coverlet on a large bed. Then Harpers converged upon us with shocked swiftness.

His mother was as calm as the ticking of the clock on the old cherry desk, but her troubled eyes slowly made the circuit from my blood-drenched dress to Troy's matted hair. "Boy—what have you done now to worry us?"

"Worry *you*?" Troy muttered. "It looks like *I'm* the one who got hit!"

"I would rather it had been me. What happened? I'm glad Dad isn't here right now. Don't you see how this will make him feel? Don't you know what people will say about your brawling —and about Adele for being out with someone who mixes in fights?"

"Will someone hand me a rag so I can wash my face?" Troy asked.

His mother rummaged out a frayed, clean rag. She handed it to me, and brought a basin of water. I eased around the long dark cut—past the gaping ridge of broken skin. Blood welled back as soon as I pulled the rag away.

His mother shook her head. "It will take some stitches to close that. You'd better get to the doctor. What did you do to the other fellow?"

Brothers and their families were still materializing from other rooms. All stared in silence except Mike, a lanky fellow with a sandy cowlick and lopsided grin. "Now hush your fuss, Troy," he said. "You're going to get that hard head of yours sewed up, and the sooner the better. Look, I'll run you into town, and we can leave Adele at her house along the way."

"Not me." My voice was becoming involuntary. "I started out today with this worthless, stubborn character, and I aim to stick the night out from sheer curiosity to see what happens to him!"

Now all eyes rotated my way. Slow smiles warmed the room. Troy's mother said, "If you will go along to take care of him I won't need to go." She stepped aside and drew some money from a cup. As she pressed it into Mike's hand I realized that it had probably been saved for food.

Mike and I led Troy out the front door. "I don't need to lean on anyone," he grumbled.

"Will you please keep quiet?" I pulled open a car door. "Now you get in this back seat with me, and hush your complaining."

As we jolted down the familiar dirt road to town a purple wave of night rolled in from the east.

"Put your head back in my lap!" I ordered.

Mike began to speak of Troy in a dry voice. "Old Troy has really had a rugged day."

"He has?"

"Sure. He couldn't eat dinner, or even sing to the girls. He got out his guitar, but his voice got all choked up. He got mad and stomped off to the river—alone. Mom got worried about him and tracked him down. She found him sitting, staring out over the water—"

Troy raised his head. "You tell the rest of that, Mike Harper, and I'll throw you out of here!"

Mike ignored him. "Troy tries to hide it, but he is really the tenderheartedest one of the whole bunch."

"This gets very interesting," I murmured.

"He always does keel over when anyone gets hurt. Can't stand the sight of blood—won't even butcher a calf and eat the meat."

"You shut up!" Troy pulled his head from my lap.

"Really loves flowers, and pretty things. Told me once he was afraid to like them too much, though, because it hurts to give up things you like. He is always hunting hard books to borrow and read, and takes up for the women of the family. Yes, sir—old Troy is sure going to make somebody a nice *wife*."

The lights of the county-seat town halted this lethal conversation. There was a race to a telephone to call a certain doctor. Only a muttered few words of explanation enlightened this ex-

Virginia gentleman when he appeared at the door of his office.

"Horse threw me all the way across the corral," Troy gasped. "You don't need to mention it to anyone."

"Funny how many accidents you boys in that part of the county run into," the doctor murmured. "I ought to report some of them to the sheriff."

"Not this one. I'll handle this one myself." Troy's face was almost as white as the sheet on the examining table. "Leave off the pain killer."

The doctor cleaned and swabbed and sewed for a time which seemed hideously long. I suddenly realized what Troy's mother had meant when she said she would rather have been the one who was hurt. I kept biting my lips because I could feel the thrust of the needle. But at last there was the merciful gleam of a bandage across the dark hair.

When we loaded in the car I expected the bandaged head to go back in my lap. But the patient drew against one corner of the seat, and turned toward the window.

"You really should put your head down," I offered. "The doctor said you had a concussion, you know. You are supposed to live a very quiet life for several weeks. You should stay out of the hot sun and avoid all excitement. That will be a terrible kind of life for you."

"I intend to hunt up a certain fellow in the morning, settle with him, and sand-furrow cotton in the afternoon," he replied tersely. "But at least this day has been good for one thing. It has taught me that you and I must not see each other again."

"What made you decide that?" I asked slowly.

"There is this attraction between us—don't deny but that you feel it too. But I am bad for you—I was a fool to dream anything else." His hands suddenly clenched together. "That's what happens when a man dares to set his sights too high." His voice broke just a little. "You were made for that poetry and music of yours—not a washtub. You know that I can't offer you anything but myself, and that's not enough. So go away as you had planned —go away so far that my boots can't keep on trailing you down."

"And what will you do?"

"It shouldn't ever matter to you. Forgive me for this mess today. That's what happens when you mix with a raw, primitive character. Let it be a lesson to you. Find you some mannerly town man with enough money to buy you an easy life. I'll apologize to your dad tomorrow."

"You—apologize to anyone?"

"Of course. What sort of person did you think I am?"

I turned to say something. It was no use. Troy crumpled forward and hit the floor board with a thud!

"Mike—Mike. Stop the car and help me! I'm afraid Troy is going to die!"

"Give 'em a shake." Mike turned his head casually. "Harpers don't die till they hit eighty or ninety. Oh yes; there was one back in Missouri who tried to sneak out of the Jesse James gang—he died young! But I told you old Troy couldn't stand the sight of blood."

I moved that dark, still head over into my lap. I glanced thoughtfully at the sky, dusted over now with whole galaxies of stars. I contemplated the most drastic thing I could think of.

I kissed that boy and I didn't try to rush through it.

It revived him all right. Too quickly! People who have just fainted are not supposed to be so downright responsive.

"Troy Harper, you big faker," I whispered.

"Good Heavens—" he gasped, "where did you get *your* practice? Why you could show those Shepherd's Crossing girls a thing or two, I grant you that." He shook his head and laughed merrily in my ear. "You just put yourself in the hands of a good teacher, and there's no telling how far you might go!" He grabbed me with both arms and caught his breath. "I warned you what it was like when a Harper set his head on a woman! I had to scheme around and find out whether you cared one thing for me." He chuckled. "You kissed me—that's my answer and I won't take any other.

"People have warned me that we wouldn't live together six months. They say there's too much to push us apart. I'll show them they are crazy!"

"Hold on here!" I put my fingers against his warm lips. "You are getting away ahead of the conversation. There's plenty between us that needs ironing out."

"You bet your life there is! So much that we'd better get started soon, or it'll take us more than a lifetime to get finished! But first of all, let me see about that teacher you would enjoy. I know just the young man who will take the job. And the charges —they can be paid in long installments over a number of years—"

The past was gone. The present flooded upon me with the never-failing scent of mesquite flowers. The bloom in my arms was fragile; it would surely fade. But it would come again, for the roots of the tree were deep. And some lovely things, even in memory, leave a fragrance which lingers through a whole year— or a lifetime.

The Visitors

Janie had been cooking less and less of her dwindling food supply for several days before she began to feel really hungry. But finally a wave of weakness came that made her sit down quickly in the hide-bottomed chair beside the kitchen window. She gazed uncertainly at the Western Texas scene outside: a mesquite tree with its mottled pattern of sun and shadow, hills folding into a cleft of purple ravines.

The patter of horses' hooves in front of the house pulled Janie unsteadily to her feet. She walked through the bare front room, past the iron bedstead and the old wooden dresser. She paused on the rotting front porch and waved to the dark-haired boy reining the bay horse.

"Oh, Rod." She smiled, and pushed back her long brown hair. "I haven't much dinner cooked yet. I didn't think you would finish branding calves so early."

"Sure." Rod's sober eyes met her own. He swung easily down from the saddle and looped the leather reins over a post. "Foreman turned us loose; told us to go home and eat." He shook his head. "I sure didn't let on that we had nothing at home to cook."

"Rod—" she frowned, "don't talk that way! You know we have pinto beans!"

"Yes, but what about bread?" He cupped her soft, round face in his slim brown hands. "Janie—Janie, honey. When you slipped off and married me your folks warned you that you would go hungry. Now, just a few months later, you *are* hungry."

"No, I'm not." She placed a hand over his. "And besides—the ranch boss pays you tomorrow. I can go to town and get a lot of groceries."

His mouth tightened at the corners. "I ought to draw my money today," he mused. "But I sure hate to let anyone know we're hungry. If we can just get by until tomorrow, everything will be all right."

Janie went back to the kitchen and shook the grate of the wood stove. But just as she started to pick up some mesquite chips a sound made her glance out the window. A familiar car was chugging down the sandy lane toward the house. Her face lost all its color.

"Oh—Rod!" She called in a stricken voice. "Here comes Mother and Dad!"

He looked up. "Well, it's high time. They haven't been none too friendly."

"But oh, Rod!" she cried. "They mustn't find us here!"

"Why?" He frowned. "Don't you want to see 'em?"

"Oh, sure," she moaned. "But Rod—they're coming right at dinnertime!"

He flushed. "Well, let's make 'em welcome to what we have."

"But listen—" she whispered wildly, "I don't have bread to cook! They'll be mad at you—really mad! They'll think— They were just beginning to get over us marrying— Oh, listen, we must do something!"

"There's nothing we can do. They're almost here."

"I know it. Oh, please!" She grabbed him by the arm. "Do what I say! Come to the clothes closet in the side room. Get in!"

"It won't work. I never heard of such a thing!" He followed her to the little room, where bright feed sacks were hung over a small closet.

"We must! Stand back here with me and be quiet. They'd see us if we tried to leave out the back door. Oh—please!"

"Whatever you say," he whispered. He put an arm around her trembling shoulders.

The car ground to a stop outside. "Let me out of here, Rupert," Mrs. Parker said to Janie's father. "This chicken and dressing is spilling in my lap." She moved her ample frame around. "Them peach pies in back is sure shook up. These is the worst roads I ever seen. I *told* Janie she was moving to the back side of nowhere when she lost her head over that boy and married him. Reckon they are here?"

"Bound to be, Mother." Mr. Parker opened the car door. "Got his horse tied here."

They stepped out. Mrs. Parker groaned as she eased up the front steps, and Mr. Parker knocked. "Wonder why they don't answer? They ought to be here. It's about dinnertime."

"Janie. Jan—ie, baby!" Mrs. Parker called. She shook the front door and pushed it back a crack. "They're not here." Her face clouded over. "I've sure been wanting to see that girl of mine. She was the best girl I ever raised. Them sure are rough roads to ride over for nothing."

"Let's bring our dinner in and wait a minute. They might show up."

Mrs. Parker carried her pan full of chicken into the kitchen and sniffed. "Not a thing cooked but a stewer of beans." She took off her slat bonnet and poked around into the cupboards. "She's out of groceries. They must have gone to town with somebody to buy some." She drew a chair away from the table and sat down. "I wish you'd look how clean everything is. I always did teach my girls how to be clean. But Rupert—" she shook her head as she looked around the kitchen—"it nearly breaks my heart to see little Janie with nothing to keep house with. Not even a linoleum down on her floors. It's not decent to have no linoleums down."

Mr. Parker chuckled. "If that's so, I can recall a time when you wasn't decent neither! Do you remember when we first married, and we was renting that place over on Hackberry Creek—?"

Mrs. Parker reddened. "Now that was different, and you know it! Why, our Janie was the prettiest girl around. Instead of marrying a ranch hand, she could have married someone like Jeff Summers, who *owned* a ranch!"

"I dunno," Mr. Parker answered. "Never took to Jeff much, myself. Saw him cuss and kick a cow once. A man who does that ain't fit to live with."

Mrs. Parker stood up. "Those kids may not be back for hours. We might as well eat a bite before we start back." She walked over to the shelves and started lifting down plates. "We should have bought Janie dishes instead of that silverware. She doesn't have much here."

"Well—" Mr. Parker took the plate she handed him—"hers are a sight prettier than the tin plates we started out with!"

"Rupert—" Mrs. Parker whirled around—"I wish you'd shut up! You're always dragging up something I forgot long ago!"

"Maybe," he answered. "Pass Janie's stewer of beans over. They'll help me remember when we ate beans—and were glad to get them! I'd trade off all my farms to start over again. Would you?"

The meal was over. Mrs. Parker covered the food and rinsed the few dishes. Then she wrote a note to Janie and slipped it under a glass.

"We better go."

"You didn't answer my question," Mr. Parker reminded her. "What question?"

"Whether you'd be willing to start over with me or not."

She frowned. "What makes you tease me that way?" Her voice softened. "Now, Rupert, you know that I would."

The car chugged away. In the closet, Janie began to move her cramped legs. Her eyes were wide; her cheeks were stained where tears had streaked down them.

"They're gone," she choked.

Rod walked beside her into the kitchen. He looked at the pan of chicken, crispy brown and smelling of sage. Silently he put his head down into his hands.

"Look up at me," Janie begged. "They brought it to us. Please —it's late. Let's eat something. They'd want you to have the chicken, Rod—you know that you're welcome to eat it."

Finally he smiled. "It's a funny thing," he answered, "but I really believe that I am."

Encounter beside the River

October had captured the whole river and thrown a light purple veil across it. The river had captured me long ago; so it was not surprising upon this fall morning to find us together again. My two children sat beside me in a red pickup, and we skimmed across a road where the shinnery country buckled down to rock bluffs.

At the edge of a cow-riddled barley field I turned the pickup from the main road and switched off the key. Far down the uncertain road another battered vehicle was coming to meet me. I recognized it as belonging to a certain Mr. Clanton, who lived where canyons emptied into the river.

Superficial history of the Clanton family flashed through my mind. I remembered how, for some years, my friends from the more prosperous upland country had been quizzical about my river neighbors. The Clanton family, I had been discreetly informed, was the most disreputable of all! They would surely swarm in with the gusto of hungry grasshoppers, eat me out of groceries, and proceed to get all interesting bounty located. Something would happen to all the gasoline around the place, that violin of mine, the typewriter, those English things, and perhaps even some of my worn pieces of furniture.

But nothing had. The Clantons came and went, borrowed what they needed, and returned it in good condition. It was true that Clanton feet sometimes rested under my table, but I could always toss in an extra handful of pinto beans for soaking.

Now I could see Mr. Clanton's face—the lean, lonesome face of an eternal exile—looking out the car window. There also were Mrs. Clanton's tanned little features—features stoical for so long that now they failed to register any emotion at all. But vulnerable indeed were the sensitive faces of the young people in the back seat. I had a sickening feeling when I realized that people hunted Scurry County treasure only underground.

"Hello," Mr. Clanton said. "You having trouble? Be glad to help you."

"Not a bit of trouble with the pickup." I laughed. "But I just can't stay away from the river; that's my main trouble in this life."

He grinned. I noticed how the gray was blotting out the black in his hair, and how tired his eyes seemed. "It's a good place to be," he answered. "Look—you've got a little time. Why don't you go over to my patch and get a watermelon?" Some of the weariness lifted from his glance. "I bet you folks got no watermelon, 'cause you missed that September shower."

"We haven't even one melon," I admitted, "but I'm afraid you can't spare any of yours."

"Oh, yes, we can!" He nodded his shaggy head. "We got plenty to spare to you! Your man—he takes me to town when my car won't run. And do you know what? He sits up there beside me like he was proud to be seen with me in town! I want to give you some watermelon. They are small now, so take two."

"I would love to have your watermelon," I smiled.

"Look by the corn patch. We have to go pull boles, or I would get them for you. Now you be sure and get two melons. One is for you and the boy and girl. Another is for the man. He can eat a whole melon! Don't take just one, now. Please take two!"

He drove away. Under the delighted urging of my children I

turned the pickup back into the road. One mile later I surveyed the cotton field rented by Mr. Clanton, and shook my head.

"I don't even see a corn patch, much less a watermelon patch. We're on a cold trail. Let's drive on past his house and down to the river."

Excuses were forthcoming. "No, Mother, we'll meet a panther down there! Let's hunt a watermelon!"

"Nonsense, a panther won't hurt you; worry about rattlesnakes!"

So past the Clanton house we jogged—past the gaiety of Mrs. Clanton's carefully hoarded zinnias and the drabness of the two-room house itself. But the stark house had compensations nudging the back door. There was a scope of hill and river, with the clean smell of cedars to flood the whole scene. An abrupt rise brought us the sight of a placid body of water which reflected the cool bulk of a bluff. Maidenhair fern clung to a grotto along the shadowy base.

"I'm so hungry for watermelon," one child sighed.

"Children! We come to this peaceful, lovely place so that Mother can think, and all you can think of is a watermelon!"

"But it's almost dinnertime. And Mr. Clanton said to get two."

I reconsidered. "Very well. He did insist."

We retraced our steps leisurely, and I studied the whole Clanton field more thoroughly. "This must be the half-dead corn patch. I don't see how there could be a live watermelon patch in that droughty spot."

I stepped across a green strip of cotton, and the whole pattern unfolded before me. Laced across the sand-blasted corn patch was a tangle of wilted watermelon vines, some meager black-eyed peas, and long rows of lank-podded butter beans. This was the Clanton garden.

What interested me most were the tracks through it. Paths were hammered into the red sand along the corn rows and worn up and down around the pea vines. I remembered hearing that the Clanton family had no more credit at the grocery stores—a local calamity for anyone! So the family had lived all summer on what these rows had produced.

Now they were failing. Even the watermelons were almost gone—there wern't more than five edible melons lying around. The little ones were becoming gourd-necked and rotten from the drouth.

"Which ones do you want, Mother?"

"Don't take any at all. Mr. Clanton can't spare these melons."

"But he said to take two—please! And we never took anything at all from him—ever."

I stood perfectly still for a moment. Had anyone ever taken anything at all from Mr. Clanton? Had he ever been able to give the neighbors anything?

There was an instinct in the man which ran deeper than continual taking.

I pulled one melon loose from the vine. Then another, gently. I handed one to my small boy. "Carry it carefully, now. Don't drop it and spoil it, whatever you do! Mr. Clanton will see our tracks and know that we got our melons. He'll be glad. We'll go now. But I'm coming back—tomorrow."

Peace

The east-bound train swayed around a Texas mountain pass. The coach seat scratched Paul Moran's lean young bones, jerking him from one realm of consciousness to another. In the first level lurked a tangled dream which he longed to put forever from his mind. In it Paul limped along a road toward a twisted backdrop of Korean mountains—alone, well aware of his isolation from members of his defeated company.

Sodden rain had turned to snow, covering the signs of battle. Even the distant guns were muffled by the drifting snow.

His recent escapes were forgotten in the press of immediate needs. He was soaked and freezing and hungry. He needed rest —in some place with a blessed fire and rags to hold the warmth against his body.

Ahead was the skeleton of a village. No dogs barked; no children shouted in the icy air. Paul moved cautiously.

He tested one house; withdrew his numbed hand when roof tiles splattered down. Farther on stood a house which seemingly had survived the bombings. More ornate than most, it had a stone fence, an entranceway, a once-charming courtyard. But as he inched toward the house Paul's brow pulled into a frown. It was only an empty hull, with blackened holes for windows. A fire bomb had destroyed everything inside.

Paul stiffened. He was not alone. A woman rose from the shadows around the carved doorway. She was not young. She was more the age of Paul's own mother. Paul stared. What was she doing here? All civilians were supposed to have evacuated long ago. Her features were drawn, and so pale that her skin appeared faintly blue. Hers was the face of an animal which had crawled to a familiar place to die. Paul faltered in choppy Korean, "Who are you?"

No answer. If the woman heard she gave no sign. She stared past him with a blankness beyond all misery, a blankness which cradled no new beginning. Vast pity engulfed Paul—a pity pleading to do something: to pick up scattered stones and prop the undermined walls, to replant the garden and clear the broken cisterns. Suddenly he knew there was nothing he could do— nothing but stumble away to hide in the hills until he was killed or captured.

The dream slithered away. Paul tugged at his uniform and raked one hand sleepily across the beard-shadow on his face. Inside the train was impersonal darkness filled with drowsing strangers; outside was the vacuum of night. The train wheels clicked on toward the hills of home.

Paul gazed out the grimy window, but saw none of the heavy blackness. Nostalgic vision blinded him, as often it had on the battlefield. He remembered mesalike hills, and the green flame of mesquite lapping through valleys to the smoke of distant cap rocks. There had been running creeks, loaded pecan trees, tall gramma grass, and fat cattle. Cotton heavy with bloom—houses stocked with provisions—laughter, pocket money, and fiddle music. It was a good world—a bountiful world—at peace.

The conductor came by. "Better get some sleep, soldier."

"I can sleep when I get home." A smile sponged the weariness from Paul's face.

"Want anything to eat, then?"

"I can eat, too, when I get home," Paul answered.

"Been in Korea?"

"Yes."

"Thought so. All you boys got a certain kind of look." The conductor's light found Paul's ticket. "Sabinal? You sure that's the right place? How long since you seen that country?"

"Three years."

"But haven't they wrote you—about how it is there, now?"

A quizzical frown creased Paul's forehead. "No. They couldn't write me. I've been in a prison camp."

Dawn fired the country west of Sabinal. Paul stirred from another troubled sleep. He raised the window in order to look out searchingly. The countryside was becoming discernible, and each horizon edge was shrouded with maroon smudge. Wind screamed through the open window. A girl across from Paul grabbed her hat with irritation.

"Sand!" Paul whistled softly. It wasn't natural looking for August; it wasn't right. The mesquite trees were ragged waifs; the grass, dry straw. No cattle rose to graze. Buzzards wheeled across the sky. Hills were shifting into correct places as the engine probed the rails toward the squat sandstone and frame buildings of Sabinal, the county-seat town.

His parents were standing beside the stucco station—Virgil Moran's face like tanned saddle leather; fresh gray streaks in his mother's hair. Paul reached for her and caught a whiff of talcum, vanilla flavoring, and an indescribable odor of growing flowers. His dad smelled of cedar smoke, Duke's tobacco, creosote dip, and cheap hair oil. Paul slowly let go of the older man's crushing handclasp.

"When we got your cablegram—" Lucy blinked rapidly and finally smiled, "we didn't know what to think! I got right down and thanked the Lord, you can be sure of that!"

"Now, Mother." Virgil cleared his throat. "No use to take on right here at the depot!"

"You look here," Lucy answered, "it's not every day that I have a boy come back from the dead! I wanted to turn it in to the *Sabinal Herald*," she continued with indignation, "and get you a big write-up in the paper, but Dad here wouldn't let me!"

"Bet your life I wouldn't." Virgil straightened up. "When I make a good crop, this town bunch here falls all over me trying to be nice. But let me make a short crop, and I can't find a feller who knows me. And listen, boy, crops have been short lately. The cows are so thin they have to be propped up to get to water."

Lucy's gentle voice broke in. "Paul, I can't wait to tell you what I have in the yard for you to see. Petunias! Real petunias! They're like none you ever saw before. Ruffled kinds—in all the softest colors: lavender, yellow, white, and rose. You've no idea how hard it's been to save them. I boarded up the west side with planks, and I sneaked out water to them every day."

Paul looked about. "When have you had rain last? You know, it looks like we'll have a sandstorm today."

Virgil mopped his face. "It blew day before yesterday, it blew yesterday, it's sure to blow today, and apt to blow tomorrow."

Paul groped for words. "Isn't there any way to stop it?"

"Stop it?" Virgil tipped back his head and laughed loudly. "You don't talk like a Texas boy any more."

"That reminds me," Lucy interrupted, "that I left a lemon pie in the old black safe, and I forgot to cover it up good. I baked it last night while the wind quit for a while."

Virgil nudged Paul. "Have you forgot what a sandstorm is?"

"Maybe I have kinda forgotten." Paul pulled at his G.I. cap. "When you're away you remember the good things and forget the bad." He looked over at a big truckload of alfalfa pulling in at the next corner. "Dad, isn't that some cow feed?"

"Might be," Virgil admitted morosely. "Relief feed. You got to go in and swear a lot of stuff to the government before you can buy it. You'll never catch me swearing that I'm broke."

"You don't have to," Lucy said. "They can tell by looking."

Virgil fidgeted as Paul gazed at the baked earth, rising dust, and sand whipping around bleak corners of business buildings. "Come on, let's go. You got any baggage?"

"Just what I have here."

Virgil turned toward the faded car. "Want to drive, Paul?"

"You go ahead." Paul flung open a door and stumbled over an old bridle. "You used to limit me on the times I could come to town. Now you go ahead."

"And you needed it. Every time I wanted you to mend a fence or grease the windmill you were sitting down there buying ice cream for some girl. You used to keep the road hot into this joint."

Paul shoved a bottle of horse liniment with his foot and said nothing. "Look, Dad," he finally urged, "if you need feed for the cows let me buy some. I have some money with me."

"Keep your money." Virgil scowled and kicked the starter. "We haven't but ten cows left. They can rustle on the river. Always did say cows didn't need to be pampered. I wouldn't have that blamed feed if they gave it me! I told everybody what would happen when they elected them Republicans. Every time there's Republicans in Washington, Texas gets in a mess. Now even the governor is in cahoots with them. If it's the last thing I ever do I'm going to throw that bird out of office!"

"I met up with some Republicans in Korea," Paul broke in. "Fact is—they acted just like plain American Democrats. Some ended up in the same compound I was in. They were decent guys."

"Don't mention Democrats to me!" Virgil let the car stop in the middle of the street and turned off the key. "The thieving, underhanded, Communist rascals! They got things in the mess it's in!"

Paul turned to his mother, perplexed. "Then what is he now?"

Virgil ignored the frantic honking of the car behind. "You mean to tell me, boy, that you never heard of the Texas Regulars?"

Paul smiled. "Some sort of National Guard outfit?"

"Could be," Virgil nodded. "We're out to whip both Republicans and Northern Democrats." He stuck his head out the window. "What does that Mexican mean, trying to crowd by? He'll wreck us. You can't teach a Mexican how to drive!"

Paul studied his father. "I knew a Mexican ambulance driver in Korea. He could drive the best I ever saw. Look here, Dad, let's get out of the middle of the street and go home."

"Let's!" Lucy insisted. "I wanted Paul to see the house before the sand got back in."

The road home was rutted and obscure. Virgil had a choice of plowing through sand or bouncing over chugholes. "Why don't you do something about this road, Dad?" Paul asked abruptly. "It reminds me of Korea—North Korea, at that."

He thought of a day before. The train had been passing through rich California agricultural lands. The sun had beamed upon ripening vineyards, rich fields of alfalfa, and ditches brimming with water. At one stop he had stepped out to buy some grapes. The lushness of the greenery in the town, the obvious prosperity, had pressed upon him. Now it all came back to him with force.

"Dad," he ventured, "when I passed through California I saw some right pretty country. Fat cattle, too. Those people out there have every convenience you could want. They seem to work together and they all have plenty of money. And the farmhouses —you should see the farmhouses!"

Virgil whipped around. "Look here, Paul, I wouldn't have that California country if you gave it to me! A good cow won't grow where a mesquite won't grow. You can't rope me in on that California stuff!"

"Have you ever seen California, Dad?"

"Nope, and I don't aim to!" Virgil's voice rose.

Paul grinned wryly and shook his head. "Might do you good, Dad, to get out and see something else for a change."

Virgil bristled. "That's the trouble with a lot of guys," he said. "When they come back from the Army they're never satisfied. They want something soft and easy."

Paul's jaw whitened. He tasted grit between his teeth. "Does he go on like this all the time?" he asked his mother. "I'd forgot."

"Some guys—" Virgil tossed another challenging glance— "think trouble was invented when *they* were born. You know what our house stands on, boy? A Comanche boneyard. How do you reckon it got there? Why, when Grandpa Moran first came here a big Indian headquarters was pitched between our yard fence and the creek. Do you reckon the Comanches turned over title to our land without a fuss?"

Paul changed the subject. "One good thing about this road— you'd never have a wreck. You can't drive fast enough."

The car jogged on. Gentle hills fell away to a long valley

where pencil lines of creeks fed into a pecan-bordered river. "Don't be surprised," Paul's mother gently warned, "when you see that the river isn't running. The fish are all dead. The pecan trees are still living, but trees around the house aren't doing so well. The orchard—is dead."

"The orchard—dead? But haven't you watered it?"

"You see, Son, the water level has lowered in our mill. It can turn for a full hour and not pump more than a bucketful. We still get enough for us and the cows to drink, and I sneak out some for the petunias."

"Listen here, Mother," Virgil broke in, "haven't I told you the water hasn't fallen in our windmill? All it is, some of those blame locust trees have pushed their roots down and caved in the well. Paul, I may get you to climb down in the well and work it over."

Paul lifted one eyebrow. The car turned up an ungraded lane, stopping before a big plank double gate. He leaped out, pushed back the gate, and clung to the car fender for the last hundred yards.

The car wheezed to a stop in front of the house. Paul drew a deep breath. The place was ravaged by sand—sand sweeping across sagging fences—sweeping across the Indian grindstone walk his mother had so carefully arranged—beating against tattered shrubs and skeleton mesquites and dying vines. It whined around the long peeling porch.

Lucy climbed out. "My petunias are on the east side, Paul. That's to keep the late sun off them." Eagerly she led him around the porch. All at once Paul felt his mother's small rough hand jerk back.

Then he saw what had stopped her.

A lean, hungry cow stepped leisurely from the petunia bed,

kicking over the plank barricade. A petunia, roots and all, dangled from thin, frothy lips. The cow gulped down a frilled lavender bloom.

Virgil was the first to speak. "What do you know? Eating those blamed flowers! The cows must be hungrier than I thought. Say, Paul, do you reckon a flower like that would poison a cow?"

"Mother?" Paul asked. "Mother—do you feel all right?"

"I'm all right," she answered vacantly.

"Dad," Paul chided, "you could fix a few fences. With all your talk, look at that rusty wire. Might as well run the cow back through the fence—it won't hurt either of them."

"Are you out of your mind?" Virgil bellowed. "Driving a good cow back through a bob-wire fence!"

"Run along," Paul waved at him. "Go on in with Mother. I'll manage out here." He stepped to the bed of mangled petunias.

"What you aiming to do?" Virgil watched him curiously.

Paul knelt beside the flower bed. He lifted one shredded plant. "I don't believe they are all gone. Look, this white one can be saved. If I carried in rock, and walled this with rock—"

"What you talking about?" Virgil asked. "Wall *what* with rock? You aim to sit out here in the sand and work on a flower bed? You'd waste more time fooling with flowers than you used to waste on girls!"

"Just let me change my clothes," Paul interrupted. "I have an idea that dishwater could be filtered through rock and sand for watering the flowers." He walked into the house, into a side room which was his own. His father followed warily.

Paul jerked down old clothing from a closet, and changed deftly into jeans and a blue shirt.

"What you doing, slamming things around?" Virgil grumbled from the doorway. "This is a peaceable place."

Paul finished buttoning up his shirt. His young dark eyes met the faded older eyes. "Then you be peaceable," he said evenly.

He went on into the kitchen, where his mother was sitting in an old chair and staring out into the tumultuous sky. "What's that I heard about some pies?" Paul asked. "I could use about half of one before I go to work."

The Hand

It was the wind which finally woke George Bennett—that wind which came bounding into El Paso before dawn like a wild mustang from the desert. It raced down the dim street beside the motel where he had stopped for the night, banging signs, twisting paloverde limbs, and kicking over garbage cans. It snorted through a crack in the window above his head, jolting his brain through shreds of fog.

"Perhaps I should let the wind come in," he considered. "At least it is something alive." But he jerked upright the side of the bed, and rolled the pane as tightly shut as the door of a casket.

He had two choices of existence now: wakefulness, where time hung upon him like a weight, and sleep—a realm torn with remembering. If only he could escape the latest dream—the one which had followed him across the long horizons from Houston. In this dream he always groped upward from his bed, hunting something real to pull him out of blackness. And then, from the shadows, a hand would reach—a hand etched with such stark reality that he knew instantly it belonged to his dead son, Ray. There were the delicate, tapering fingers—fingers which could coax music from any piano. He could feel them, warm and secure, fasten upon his own.

But just as he always began: "Where have you been, Son? Are you real? They told me you were dead—what a joke! Stay with me—help me—don't leave me again!"—the hand was gone, dissolving into the nothingness from where it had come.

George shook his head and reached for his slippers. Ray's hands, those beautiful, musical hands, would never reach for him again on this earth. They were crushed and broken and decaying, mangled by a plane carrying Army recruits, that plane he had been detailed to ride in to training camp.

George noticed his expensive topcoat, carefully arranged on a chair. Even his clothes declared his way of life: an investor, successful, self-sufficient. He still had orderly habits, even on a trip which led nowhere. He had always hated disorder, and waste—waste of things, and waste of human beings. Now he wanted to blot himself from a universe where such things could happen. Yet he would prefer to do this in a careful fashion. But how—that was the question. Clients had come to him for advice for years; he had always known the right answers. Now he did not know the only one which really mattered to him.

This trip was the only impulsive thing he had ever done, and its beginning had been commonplace. He had first decided to go to San Antonio and stay with an aunt for a week. He mentioned to friends that he needed a change—a rest. This thing—had been quite a shock. Losing his wife three years ago, and now Ray—such a tragedy could knock reason from any man. The friends had nodded wisely and told him to see something different—have a good time.

But when he started driving west suddenly there was no end to the road, yet no reason for turning back. A feeling of complete distaste, of revulsion, of seeing or talking to anyone he had ever known gripped him. He did not want to be confronted with anything familiar—ever again. He did not want to be confronted with anything at all.

So he bypassed San Antonio, scribbled excuses to the aunt, and drove steadily. Finally he realized he was crossing the Pecos River, and soon he saw waves of mountains foaming across the west. Something about the alien, stinging, empty country matched his own emptiness. There should be some quiet, neat way to dispose of himself in this sterile land.

George rose and walked to the window. The lights of Juarez, south of the Rio Grande, were beginning to fizzle like burned-out firecrackers. A streak of autumn light was touching the east, staining the adobe and cement of the town, and the mountains crouching around it. But why should he stay here? This was not reality—he had no identity with this place. He would follow the road west, to where the desert dissolved against some unknown shore.

He drove his car through the pass above the town. The valley ahead, with its irrigation ditches and cottonwood trees, slowly illumed with morning. He followed it toward the north, through little Mexican settlements with their cantinas and plastered stores. Puffs of white dust whined past salt cedars and a herd of goats. Men were walking beside the road now, brown, nondescript men carrying cottonsacks. In the half-light they were primitive creatures, as much a part of nature as the tamarisk and mesquite. He could not imagine offering one of them a ride, or beginning a conversation with him. These people might have citizenship papers, but they were no countrymen of his—they were still tied to the faceless masses of Mexico.

Now a high wire fence flanked the road on one side, guarding cotton and alfalfa and tomato fields. "Federal Correctional Institute—No Trespassing" the sign said. Work, on this prison, had something to do with correction, for the fields were carefully cultivated. A man was walking beside the road in shapeless clothing; he held out a dawn-streaked arm for a ride. George passed him, but had not gone far down the road before he felt a tire blow out on the car.

When the car swerved and bucked and spun toward the fence every fiber in him rose and fought the steering wheel. He slowed its whirling; he kept the car upright and stopped it with the brakes properly applied. This is a beautiful piece of irony, he suddenly thought. What was the idea—why did he insist upon a painless, neat end for himself—a contrast to the crescendo of horror of Ray's last moments?

The dust cleared. He slowly stepped out to look at the front tire. He hated to change tires—it was a dirty job.

Then he heard the panting of the man trotting up beside him. This was the same fellow he had passed, a Mexican—and little more than a boy. The sun, just tipping the edge of the mountains, flooded his coffee-colored face. It was sculptured in elemental lines: high cheek planes, long-lashed dark eyes, a wavy black mane of hair, and a disarming smile. George sensed a gap between himself and the face. What was it—a limited mind, education, civilization, or just sophistication?

"Señor! The car! She almost turn over! Are you hurt?"

"Not at all. Is there a gas station nearby?"

"Station? Not for several miles, Señor. But I, Luis Hidalgo, will change your tire."

"I will pay you."

Luis shrugged thin shoulders. "No—no pay. But I would like you to give me a ride several miles down the road."

"Why not?" asked George. "Sorry I passed you by the first time." He reached in the trunk, and pulled out tire tools. "Do you have a car too, Luis?" He felt abruptly relaxed, at ease, with the young man. Since there was such a gap of intellect between them there need be no effort on casual chatter.

"No, Señor, I have never owned a car. But I have been taught to do many things." Luis caressed the tire, and placed the jack underneath the car. "This is a beautiful thing, Señor. It is good to ride in such a car. People do not pick up strangers from the highway into such cars. Are you afraid—Señor?"

George Bennett drew in his breath slowly. "There is a time which comes in a man's life when it makes absolutely no difference what happens to him."

Luis fixed dark eyes upon him. "Like—Señor—when a man south of the Rio grows so hungry that he will manage to cross—that he will cross even if he walks into the guns of the Border Patrol?"

George stared back. "Like that—I suppose. You surprise me. You speak English very well—in a literate way."

"I have studied English, Señor. I have wanted to learn English more than anything in the world. Would you say I look like an American?"

"An American? Now that's a hard question. Americans come in all sizes, shapes, and colors. No, you don't look like most Americans we have around Houston, who are Anglo or German or French. You are Spanish, of course. But there are lots of Spanish-Americans here in this area."

"I wish I could be one of them," Luis murmured. "I am a Mexican national, Señor—I am not an American."

"Well, what's the difference? You get to work over here. You are better off than we are. Our country is always trying to save the world—it has obligations and a big Army to feed. It stacks up atomic bombs, pays for most of the United Nations, and scatters the bones of its people all over the world."

"Señor!" Luis spluttered in his haste. "If you knew the truth, you would not talk so. Who drives the car this morning, and who walks? I was born in a village far beyond the border. Sometimes we had corn, sometimes we did not. Then my people gnawed the barks of trees, and ate the flesh of cactus. I could not go to school, and a pair of American shoes was the greatest thing I could imagine. Look at me—if I were an American I would be the happiest man alive!"

"That's the sort of thing that is easy for you to say, but you can't prove it." George's face began to flush with the unexpected conversation. "What if you had gone to the trouble to join the Army—as my son did a few weeks ago? What if you, with mistaken nobility, had climbed into an airplane and had your life snuffed out on the way to training camp? Would it have been worthwhile?"

"Oh, Señor—I am sorry." The limpid eyes misted over. "But I still say it is better to be an American."

"You'll have a whale of a time proving to me that you would put out much effort to be one," George muttered. "But look— I've ruined this tire, and it was almost new. Get in, and we'll use the spare awhile."

Luis dusted his jeans and stepped in the door. The car hurried past acres of corn and cotton and more tomatoes. The Prison headquarters came fleeting into view, sitting more than a mile beyond the entrance gate.

"My son—" the words burst from George, "my son was a dreamer, a musician. He created beauty." George was no longer trying to phrase words Luis would comprehend, he was speaking to himself. "He was an idealist—he lived by things of the spirit. He thought—no price was too high to pay for what was right. But if we could have lived in another land, in some uncomplicated society, he would be with me yet." George felt his hands tremble on the wheel. "He would not have left me to help save the world. When nothing will ever be the same for me again—and I know it—why carry the load?"

Luis turned to him. "Señor—have you not heard that everything living must die? If death came only to Americans, it would be a strange world. But listen—in my homeland people die daily. as they do here. My father—when I was a child I saw my father thrown from a horse. His foot caught in the stirrup; the half-wild creature started circling down the mountainside, with my father's head bumping like a melon upon the ground. Señor— if you had lived near my *rancho* both you and your son might have died long ago. There are no doctors—and many sicknesses. You would not have wanted your son to live in a mud house, with no glass in the windows. Would you have wanted to drink water with the animals? Would you have enjoyed making a crop of corn with a hoe?"

"Look, Luis," George silenced him. "I suddenly realize that I haven't eaten breakfast. Have you?"

"No—nothing but tomatoes and one onion."

George chuckled. The unfamiliar sound vibrated in the car. "How do you expect to work on a diet like that? How about letting me order you some eggs and pancakes? Or maybe you eat tortillas?"

When they reached the outskirts of a village, he pulled in front of a cafe. George stepped inside and ordered eggs and toast and tortillas, and waited while the cook stirred around in the kitchen. Finally the radio began a persistent hum.

"Road blocks have been thrown around the area to apprehend an illegal alien who has escaped from the Federal Prison—"

A waitress quietly tapped George on the shoulder. She kept glancing out the glass front of the cafe. "Listen, Mister—did you pick up that Mexican national down the road? Or is he working for you?"

"How can you tell he's a Mexican national?" George asked.

She chuckled. "You must be a stranger here. You can tell those boys a mile away! They don't act like local Mexicans—they are scared and got a different look from the eyes. The Border Patrol has blocked the road just two hundred yards up—near the center of town. It might be best for you to get rid of him. He can hide out somewhere and find work."

"Thank you," George answered quietly. "Is the food ready?"

He carried the sack to the car, and handed it to Luis. "If we want to eat this," he said, "we'd better pull down some side road beyond the cafe here." He turned the car swiftly, slipped past adobe houses, and pulled around a hedge of salt cedars flanking an irrigation ditch.

"Eat all you can—you'll need it. Look, Luis, when the Prison officials and Border Patrol throw up a road block is there any way around it?"

Luis took a bite from a tortilla. A muscle twitched high upon one cheek. "Señor, that would depend. They would probably block the highway here to the north, and the road across the desert to Columbus, and the back road along the river. I do not know whether they would block the levee road along the canals. And there is a pass east across the mountains here—"

"You know this country well, don't you?"

"Fairly well, Señor. I have worked on farms here, and been down many of the roads. But whether one could get past—that would depend on how badly a person wished to."

"How badly do you want to get by, Luis?"

"Señor." He put down the tortilla, and looked into George's eyes. "Do not be afraid. I will not harm you."

"That part doesn't matter. What is your trouble? What have you done?"

"Señor—" His voice quavered. "Do not worry. I have done nothing—nothing bad. I am only a worker, and have no visa. I once had one—I used to come over and work. That is when I learned to speak English. But finally a law comes from your country which takes away my visa. When I come to Juarez the last time the men tell me the quota is full. So I wait in town a few days and can find nothing. I know that I will starve if I stay there, and I will starve if I go back to my old home. So I decide to cross the river." He trembled slightly. "Do you want to hear more, Señor?"

"Go ahead."

"So I walk along the river, and I find this place where it runs at the back of adobe houses, where I can hide. I see boys swimming in the river just before sundown. I whisper to them softly, roll up my clothing, and join them. I slip to the bank and put my clothes behind a wall. After dark I climb out, dress, and start walking down the road on the American side. I find a little store where I can buy a cottonsack, and I put it over one arm. I see a Patrol car coming, and it slows beside me. But I look straight ahead, and the officer goes on, Finally I come to a farm road where I can rest until morning. In the morning I pick up my sack and find a small patch where I can work. I tell the farmer that I am local. I do not think he believes me, but he needs a picker. Each afternoon I pretend to leave and walk to my home. I hide near the canal and eat cold food from cans. Three weeks go by, and the farmer is getting more pickers. These are American Mexicans, and they believe nothing I say. One day, while I am working, a Patrolman comes and takes me away."

"Do they send you back across the border?"

"No, not then. I am put—they call it detain—here at the Prison to work on the farm for awhile. For that I thank the God of Heaven. I am given a clean place to stay, with a real bed. I am given clothes, and a place to take a bath. I have good food to eat every day. But, Señor—the best part was yet to be! After I did my farm work each day I went to school! There were classes in English, and a man teach me to write and spell. At last—I could learn what an American knows." He unclenched his fingers slowly. "But these great gifts could not always be. My term was ending. I was to be sent across at Juarez. So then a wonderful plan came to me." He stared across the mat of salt cedar. "We were supposed to gather the last tomatoes yesterday. One of the men was sick, so we were in the patch later than the guards had planned. The guard riding his horse was at one end of the row when I saw a tractor pulling a trailer for us. I lay down in a high bunch of tomatoes. I know the other prisoners missed me, but they say nothing—I think—as they went back. Within an hour there was a great noise, and I knew I was being hunted. I lay so flat among the tomatoes that no one could find me without stepping upon me. At last they must have decided I had escaped on the highway, for they began stopping cars there. They went away just before daylight. I climbed out and began walking. Then I came upon you."

"But how can you hope to get away—to hide in the United States and not be found?"

"You do not understand, Señor. I did not dare hope that I could escape for long. I was only hoping to hide out from the

Prison long enough to cause enough trouble to get a long detain sentence this time. For you see, Señor—I do not wish to escape at all!"

"What now?"

"I get out of your car, so you will not be questioned. I will walk down the road, and the Patrol will see me, and capture me."

George drew a long breath. "I don't like to do this to you."

"*Es nada.*" Luis' white teeth flashed. "The most of my life I have been walking down roads. It is the best I can hope for. Now you, Señor, can live in your country and do many good things for its people. Maybe someday I, Luis Hidalgo, will do something for someone."

George frowned. "Luis—look. There should be a better way out of this for you."

"Do not worry, Señor. The guards know me. They will do nothing bad. And I have a guitar waiting for me in prison! Remember me when you go back to your home and work." He opened the door of the car, and stepped around to George. The wind plastered the old clothes to his lean young frame. He put out a hand—a hand scarred and stained and lined with hunger and hard work. The fingers closed on George's hand with a warm, secure grip—a lingering touch. Finally they were gone, and Luis was saying, "*Vaya con Dios, Señor.* May God always be with you."

He stepped away from the car into the road. Once he turned back and waved, then disappeared around a bend.

Canaan

Two dry years had gone by that time in Western Texas before Les Blanton began talking about some dreams of his. His talk began as slowly as water simmering in a coffeepot over a mesquite fire up the Colorado River. But, just as the water in a coffeepot, it finally boiled over.

"I wonder if there isn't a country better than this somewhere?"

The men sitting on the porch of the community store turned toward him, causing a mild rustle. They had retreated an hour ago to this patch of shade; now darts of sunlight pointed toward their boot toes. One man was as stiffened as the gray boards above him; the others moved as lithely as wildcats in the brush. Les Blanton was somewhere in between—he had half-grown children who would rather sneak off to town than ride pasture. His skin was the color of old leather; his lean hands were scarred from rope burns and cottonstalks. His jeans sagged around the waist; his black hat was slowly decaying.

Les's friend Tucker Westfall sat silently thinking while the oldest man in the group spoke.

"Oh, calm down, Les! It'll rain someday, when the cotton is ready to gather. Even if you landed in Heaven, you wouldn't feel at home there. You're too used to sand-furrowing cotton, freezing in a norther, doctoring sick calves, drinking gyp water, dodging cyclones, burning up in the summertime, and going back to the bank looking pitiful when the year is over."

"I might get used to something else, fast," Les answered drily.

"I was over west, above the Cap Rock, last summer. Farmers around Lamesa were drilling a bunch of new water wells. The land was black, and level as a table—not rolling and washed-away like our country here. The people who kept cows penned 'em in feed lots and didn't have to chase through cedar breaks to scare them out. The houses was nice—all painted white with flowers and grass around. My woman could have plenty of water there to keep things clean, and a washing machine for her clothes."

"Get such notions out of your head," the old man interrupted. "In my lifetime I've seen a lot of men who move around. All they do is spend money and wear themselves out. You'll never find anything perfect, anywhere. I don't reckon it was planned that way for this earth. If things were better we might want to stay around too long. In one country there are one set of drawbacks— in another country others. You'll learn about the plains around Lamesa—if you live there. You better stay where you already know what the troubles are all about! Settle back and watch for a cloud bank in the northwest. My cotton is blooming on top of the stalk."

"So's mine," Les answered. "You watch for rain all you please —I'm through. I'm going to leave this country as soon as I can."

The men sitting around Les paid no more attention to his threat than to the sound of dry maizestalks rattling in the wind. For he had a fair piece of land rented, there in the upper forks of the river. The cotton land, back from draws and arroyos, was deep sand—the mellow red kind which would hold moisture around roots during dry weather. The hills above the river grew good buffalo and mesquite grass—when it rained. And, luckily for Les, he didn't have a landlord who came snooping around much. This owner was a storekeeper in the county seat, and too busy with his schemes there to come out to the farm and tell Les what he ought to do. Neither did he come to see if the house needed new window lights or boards where the roof leaked, but that was to be expected.

When Les turned the land back to him at renting time, in August, his eyes narrowed for a moment. Then he recovered, and cleared his throat. "Well, I expect I won't have no trouble renting it to any of a dozen fellows." His glance kept running over the store while he talked to Les, singling out customers from people who were just looking around. "People come to me all the time, begging to rent land."

"Then let one of the poor devils have it," Les replied. He stalked out of the store with his head up, feeling more free and proud than he had in a long, long time.

Once Les was settled on the plains, news of him filtered back through the familiar grapevines of kinfolk and neighbors. He had actually rented a little blackland farm with a square bungalow and neat outbuildings. It had a bathroom inside, and a paved road ran not far away. "I guess Les is fixed for life," people concluded in his old haunts below the Cap Rock. "He's got a good little irrigation well and some cows to feed out. I can't see him coming back here again."

Yet, three years later, he was back. Tucker Westfall did not try to hide his surprise one December morning when Les stopped by to tell him that he was moving back to the same land—into the same forsaken house.

"My old landlord was glad to get me back, too." Les closed

the door against the arctic-sharp wind. His fringed leather jacket swished softly. "Some of those starved-out cotton pickers tore boards out of the side of the house to burn. And you should see the tin cans they left on the place! Some of 'em beer cans, too."

"Boy—have you gone stark out of your mind?" Tucker handed him a chair. "You mean—you're bringing your bunch back here? After having a chance at plenty to eat, a good pickup to ride in, and nice clothes? I thought you made some money up there!"

"Sure, I made a little money," Les admitted. He fingered his new cream-colored Stetson hat. "But like someone once told me, Tucker, things were not really perfect after I got there. To begin with, I didn't fit in with those dressed-up cattle traders—and I didn't like living so close to town. My kids got lazier every day; wanted to dress up and go hang around the stores all the time.

"Our house was sitting out in plain sight of everyone; I couldn't even kick a cat out the back door without all the neighbors knowing about it. And people looked at me like I was crazy when I didn't hire Mexicans to do all my field work.

"And those fool cows! They had to be fed every bite they ate, like babies! Before long I began to feel just as penned-up in a stall as they were. Boy, am I glad to be back where I can get out of these clothes and get to work!"

For two years Les fared very well. His spirits remained high while he patched up the dismal house and cleaned out the cistern. For a while rains came and sprouted the old red pasture in the river's curve. But finally came a year so scorching that algerita berries shriveled on their limbs, and sagebrush drooped across rock crevices. Cows hunted anything green, even coarse salt grass beside the river.

One smouldering July afternoon Les joined a little group in front of the store. He fanned his sweat-drenched face, and gulped a lukewarm bottle of orange soda pop. "Boys," he asked suddenly, "don't you think there could be some country better than this, somewhere?"

Tucker turned slowly. "You find it. I don't have the energy left."

"I've found it already," Les announced calmly. "I've been reading the *Texas Almanac*, where it describes all the counties. It tells about a place where it rains in the summer—where there are mountain ridges and fertile valleys. Cattle do well on the ranges there, for it's not too hot in the summer nor too cold in the winter. There is timber on the hills, and big oak in the valleys beside the running streams."

"You sure you don't have this place mixed up with the Happy Hunting Ground?" Tucker asked.

"No, sir! It's right out there in the Davis Mountain country, west of the Pecos!"

A few days later Tucker wildly hailed Les in the road. "The big bank president Clayton wants to see you down in his office!"

"What for? My note's not due till November."

"Hold on! It looks like luck is finally going to come your way! I always did say you could handle cows better than any man around, and Clayton knows that. He caught me in town and said he had a rancher friend who died two weeks ago. His widow wants to move off the ranch and needs a good man to run it. Clayton said for you to come right in and talk to him about the job."

Les looked up blankly. "And where—where is this ranch?"

"Out in Jeff Davis County. In the Davis Mountains."

Les paled slightly. He reached for a cigarette with trembling fingers.

"I know you would be tickled to death. I told him you would hurry in."

Les blew a weak puff of smoke. "Sure," he said, "I'll go in and see him."

Two days later a puzzled Tucker made an excuse to go past Les Blanton's fence line. He found Les fixing a windmill at the edge of the sand, and drove his car as near as he could. He started talking by the time he got out of the car.

"Man, I have never been so surprised in my life over what I just heard! I thought you would be selling your cows and packing—ready to go!"

"Not so's you can tell it." Les put down a pipe wrench.

"Is it true—what I heard at the store—that you turned Clayton down on the ranch manager's job? I heard that he asked Elmer Hartley to take the job after you wouldn't have it."

"I reckon he did." Les quietly pulled up another length of rusty sucker rod. "Get hold of this here."

"I heard that Hartley was going to live at the ranch headquarters—get a good salary—a share of the profits—that it's a pretty place—"

"Maybe so. Hold this." Les stepped onto the first rung of the mill ladder. "I don't know why in the name of common sense windmill leathers always have to wear out in the middle of a hot day in a dry time. The cows will be bawling around here before I get this fixed."

Tucker looked steadily into his friend's face. "Les, what on earth ails you? It was the only chance you ever had to do something big for yourself—to make a better living for your family—"

Les glanced down. "Hush up, Tucker." He gripped another length of the ladder with his worn cotton gloves. "If you don't mind, I'd like to keep some nice country in my mind just to *think* about for the rest of my life!"

The Comanche Arrowmaker

Just beyond the Indian camp, where a cedar-choked canyon twisted toward the river, the old Comanche arrowmaker tended a mesquite fire beside the brush. He liked to draw aside from the camp, even as time had led him aside from life, so that the mildly curious would not bother him during work. And for those who were in earnest, they could always find him—the eager young brave out to draw blood with a better lance, the moon-struck lover explaining the contours of a desired red-flint bird arrow to slip to his sweetheart as a sign that his heart had been fatally pierced, the warrior out for sturdy gray flint pieces with serrated edges and curving barbs to drain away the blood of a victim.

The old man was as gnarled as a mossy old cedar, and when he moved among his flints the past footfalled beside him. He rolled another chunk of wood onto the fire. The beginning of his life was so far behind him that he could not remember it, and it seemed there would never be an ending; but this he knew—nothing was gained if the fire went out.

He had always thought of death as streaked with black—a painted Apache face darting from behind a jagged rock, with a tomahawk in upraised hand. Or he thought of death as lurking with the faceless rattlesnake where tall grass quivered, or in the whoop and din and dust of a battle. But he had never known that the hands of life could simply slip away, finger by finger, into a soft fog of forgetfulness. And he no longer tried to care, for if he began to care again an old twisted pain would come back with the need and longing. And he could not dwell upon it now, how the woman who had once cheerfully cleaned his tent and threaded sinew along the seams of his shirts was crumbling in a grave where the panther prowled at night.

But a man must take what comes. Life was a buffalo horn of water, sweet and brimming at the top, murky and bitter at the bottom, so there could be no complaint when it was taken away.

He looked at his piles of flint. Small boys had better not come chasing each other through these heaps! There was coarse gray native flint, and the translucent black from the San Saba, and flint ranging in colors from muted pastels to sooty brown, much of which had been traded from far-ranging Indian bands. There was a chunk of metal which had cost many hides from a Mexican trader, although the Old Arrowmaker had been doubtful from the start of such foreign substance. Red spots were already nibbling at the heart of the metal, while nothing but breakage could destroy a piece of flint.

Suddenly he understood, in some fading recess of his mind, why he sat and created arrowheads instead of crawling away to some corner of the camp to die, as his generation had done one by one. It was simply that he wished to make something which would last as long as the Earth-Mother lasted, so long as her husband, the sun, permitted her to glide through the heavens. And there was little that he, or any of his people, had done which was lasting. When strength had blazed under his young hide in a restless ebb and flow, he had pitched into the brunt of a battle, thrusting his spears into strong Apache throats, watching the flesh split apart, seeing the foam of death break upon the lips, hearing the last hiss from a severed windpipe. But, when all was over and his hands were dried, there was nothing but blood spots upon his shirt, stale scalps, and Apache widows wailing on some dark hill.

And it was the same with camp life, for the Comanche had taken so much buffalo inside his hide that he roamed with the same blind instinct of the beast—hunting water holes and shelters and salt licks, pitching hides for covering and then hearing the camp crier announcing where the next move would be. And there was nothing much a man could make or keep or carry for his own, for Comanches must travel as lightly as the wild duck in the dying of the seasons. And time had a way of sneaking in and stealing a man's living treasures—those creatures of flesh and blood who once wandered happily in and out the door of his tent and ate freely of his food. So finally a man could ask life to give him nothing new—he could only ask quietly that it bring back what it had already taken away.

The Old Arrowmaker rolled a chunk of silky gray flint into the coals. When it grew very hot it would split with a hiss, and thin pieces would pop many directions. He would select those pieces for working which required the least chipping to put into shape.

Suddenly two sturdy lads came racing across the brow of the hill, spurred by the noise of splitting flint. They wanted to watch the arrowmaker so that someday they might copy him and make their own arrows—with chipping as delicate as the imprint of a maiden's kiss.

The Old Arrowmaker reached with a forked stick to rake out the pieces of flint. He would show them. He had never been a greedy man—not greedy for too many shirts, too many buffalo, or too many sons. He was not even greedy—the Good God knew it—for taking more years of life than were his just share upon this earth. These later years had been put upon him not by his own desire, but by the Good One. At any time he was ready to put away his simple tools. But until he did—that notched trademark in each side of his arrowheads would show to all men who walked the earth that there once lived a man who did one thing well.

Farewell to the River

The sun was dropping toward a long mesa in the west when I finished packing the last of the large boxes. I stood and looked at the collection of furnishings, clothing, and household goods stacked about each room, ready for moving. I felt the weariness of my body seep through the marrow of my bones and filter deep into my soul. For in the morning I was leaving my home here on the Upper Colorado of Western Texas—the only real home I had ever known.

I stepped through the simple living room onto the long farm-house porch to watch my last sunset crown the cap rock. This was not a country to catch the wandering eye of a traveler and arrest it with immediate beauty; yet it was a land of infinite variety and mood—both of subtle loveliness and raw anguish. It was a land belonging to the sun and wind, bounded by a big lonely circle of sky—a land at the mercy of the elements of Heaven. It lay below the High Plains in graduations of elevation and terrain, from an occasional high point which had defied erosion, down to the depths of cedar-shadowed canyons. The Colorado, which had fought its way to the Gulf of Mexico in ages past, made a spiral through the center of my country. Its flow of water, though erratic and often salty, gave life to tamarisk and willow and scrub oak, and furnished a refuge for numberless small creatures. Back across the hills and arroyos leading to it, the green flame of mesquite trailed into the smoke of distant horizons.

I had seen the years slip across the hills: first, lightly and easily, like shadows running before the wind, then more slowly, with measured tread. I had seen the river blue and shivering in the cold of midwinter, or sparkling through the mirages of summer. I had seen numberless dawns split the sky and let the light come pouring through. I had seen clouds of stars circle the sky at night. I had seen slim young moons plunge through sprays of clouds, fat October moons bob like jack-o-lanterns in the past, and pale old moons slip like ghosts over the hills. I had walked the trails leading to the river—old Comanche trails worn by moccasined feet. I knew the secret places where maidenhair fern clung to damp ledges, and where the wily catfish fed deep in murky water. I knew when spring came laughing across the hills, with sunlight in her hair and warm Gulf winds spinning behind her. I knew the sweetness of growing things—cactus flower, algerita, wild verbenas, gramma grass. I knew the snarl of distant thunder, the taste of silver raindrops, the gleaming arc of a bow in the clouds.

I walked across the porch. Winds had scattered the towering clouds of noonday, bouncing them into the horizon's vast circle. I stepped in front of the house so that I could have a sweeping view.

Suddenly I became aware that the whole horizon was beginning to kindle with an unearthly, iridescent glow. The sun, in dipping to the west of me, had fallen behind a black little cloud, shutting its light from where I stood. But, due to some uncanny illusion, the towering thunderheads—almost all the same height —ringing the horizon around me seemed to be transformed into fountains of light gushing with rose and gold and crimson. It seemed as if the Kind Spirit of the Universe had arranged this display especially for me. I watched it silently, in awe and wonder—transfixed by this last crowning burst of beauty, climax of all the years I had known.

At last a dark wave of night began to wash away the color in the east.

A cool breeze stirred my hair and brought back reality.

"Thank you, Kind Spirit," I whispered gently. "Thank you forever."